# Walking Among Giants:
# From Elvis to Garth

# Walking Among Giants: From Elvis to Garth

*The Bobby Wood Story*

Bobby Wood
and
Barbara Wood Lowry

*Walking Among Giants*

Copyright © 2012 Bobby Wood
All rights reserved.

No portion of this book may be reproduced, stored in a retrieval system, or transmitted in any form or by any means—electronic, mechanical, photocopy, recording, scanning, or other—without the prior written permission of the publisher.

For information regarding sales or licensing, please contact the publisher:

Dunham Books
63 Music Square East
Nashville, Tennessee 37203

www.dunhamgroupinc.com

Trade Paperback ISBN 978-0-9851359-4-2
Ebook ISBN 978-0-9851359-5-9

Printed in the United States of America

# Contents

Foreword ............................................. 9

Tributes ............................................. 11

Prologue ............................................. 21

Chapter One
THE EARLY YEARS ..................................... 23

Chapter Two
FROM GOSPEL TO ROCK AND ROLL ..................... 38

Chapter Three
MEMPHIS—A NEW BEGINNING ......................... 48

Chapter Four
GALLIPOLIS, OHIO—NEW RELATIONSHIPS ............... 56

Chapter Five
A NEW SONG ......................................... 59

Chapter Six
A LIFE-CHANGING MOMENT .......................... 63

Chapter Seven
A TRIP BACK HOME ................................... 70

Chapter Eight
Studio Time in Memphis . . . . . . . . . . . . . . . . . . . . . . . . . . . . . . 73

Chapter Nine
The Hit Factory . . . . . . . . . . . . . . . . . . . . . . . . . . . . . . . . . . . . . 80

Chapter Ten
Memories from the Sound Room . . . . . . . . . . . . . . . . . . . . . 84

Chapter Eleven
Learning the Ropes . . . . . . . . . . . . . . . . . . . . . . . . . . . . . . . . . 88

Chapter Twelve
The Comeback of Elvis Presley . . . . . . . . . . . . . . . . . . . . . . . 91

Chapter Thirteen
A Reflection on Family . . . . . . . . . . . . . . . . . . . . . . . . . . . . . 101

Chapter Fourteen
A Business Like No Other . . . . . . . . . . . . . . . . . . . . . . . . . . 106

Chapter Fifteen
It's Time to Move . . . . . . . . . . . . . . . . . . . . . . . . . . . . . . . . . . 110

Chapter Sixteen
A Band Connection . . . . . . . . . . . . . . . . . . . . . . . . . . . . . . . . 114

Chapter Seventeen
Days with Garth Brooks . . . . . . . . . . . . . . . . . . . . . . . . . . . . 118

Chapter Eighteen
Getting the Right Sound . . . . . . . . . . . . . . . . . . . . . . . . . . . 134

Chapter Nineteen
Recognizing a Hit Song . . . . . . . . . . . . . . . . . . . . . . . . . . . . 137

Chapter Twenty
A Friend for Life . . . . . . . . . . . . . . . . . . . . . . . . . . . . . . . . . . 142

Chapter Twenty-One
The Lord Must Be First . . . . . . . . . . . . . . . . . . . . . . . . . . . . 145

Chapter Twenty-Two
What Newcomers Need to Know . . . . . . . . . . . . . . . . . . . . 148

Chapter Twenty-Three
Darker Days—Lonely Days—Wrong Choices . . . . . . . . 151

Chapter Twenty-Four
Nashville Sound—Memphis Soul. . . . . . . . . . . . . . . . . . . . 155

Chapter Twenty-Five
Memphis Boys—Worldwide Fame . . . . . . . . . . . . . . . . . . . 157

Chapter Twenty-Six
Talking About the Hits . . . . . . . . . . . . . . . . . . . . . . . . . . . 161

Chapter Twenty-Seven
Stars Past and Present . . . . . . . . . . . . . . . . . . . . . . . . . . . 164

Chapter Twenty-Eight
A Conversation with Bobby and T.G. Sheppard . . . . . . 168

Chapter Twenty-Nine
The Highwaymen . . . . . . . . . . . . . . . . . . . . . . . . . . . . . . . . 172

Chapter Thirty
True Legends. . . . . . . . . . . . . . . . . . . . . . . . . . . . . . . . . . . . 175

Chapter Thirty-One
The Desire to Write . . . . . . . . . . . . . . . . . . . . . . . . . . . . . 178

Chapter Thirty-Two
On the Road—In the Studio . . . . . . . . . . . . . . . . . . . . . . 181

Chapter Thirty-Three
The Memphis Boys Today . . . . . . . . . . . . . . . . . . . . . . . . . 185

Chapter Thirty-Four . . . . . . . . . . . . . . . . . . . . . . . . . . . . . . . . 187

Epilogue
Another stage. Another show. . . . . . . . . . . . . . . . . . . . . 190

# Foreword

If you browse through the greatest recordings in history, you will find one name appearing again and again—Bobby Wood. Bobby Wood has left his mark on this world one lick at a time. Allen Reynolds introduced me to Bobby in the fall of 1988, and even during the very first session, Bobby's "gift" was apparent. His ability to create memorable hooks of soul and simplicity explains his success in all music genres. Every artist loves Bobby for his diversity. Not only in style, but his diversity in instruments. Bobby is known for his piano work, but he is equally known for his B3, Wurlitzer, and Synth performances. Add on to that his talent for songwriting and producing, and you have a simple explanation why Bobby Wood may very well be the most successful musician to grace the music business for the last five decades! But Bobby himself will tell you he did not do it alone. First, and foremost, he is a man of great character and faith. It is his faith in God that has underpinned his life and work and continues to do so.

*Walking Among Giants* is the story of a man who never gave up in spite of discouragement and tragedy. It is the true story of a man who not only believes in miracles, but who has also lived them. It is moving, often heart wrenching, but always inspiring. It is the story of a man who is living the American dream in the world of music. It is a story of a man of unbending faith. It is the story of Bobby Wood, the common thread that winds among the giants of our time.

**– Garth Brooks**

# *Tributes*

To really know Bobby Wood and to understand the magnitude of his talents, you must first talk to the people who have worked with him over his half-century in music. And here is what some of them have to say about this music legend:

*"Let me start by saying, "I love Bobby Wood." As a father, you will not find someone more proud of his children and grandchildren. As a husband, he and Janice have been a couple to envy. As a player, there is no one else remotely like him. As a friend, his love has been solid as a rock.*

*"Bobby Wood is one of those artists that make everyone around him rise to a new level. His heart and soul are in every note that he plays. His appreciation for music has made him not only a great player, but a great producer, writer, and arranger. His understanding of space makes the notes he plays special and defining. He is 'taste.'*

*"This business comes down to one thing—selling records. I bet Bobby Wood has played on more records sold than any other player…bar none."*

— **Garth Brooks**
*Music Legend*

"If there's a Super Band in the music business, keyboard artist Bobby Wood is on the A-Team. I had the good fortune of working with him on my third album, which included his favorite, 'Why Me,' and later with the Highwaymen—among the most soulful and satisfying experiences of my life.

"Thank you, Bobby, for the heart and soul you put into our music."

– **Kris Kristofferson**
*Recording Artist, Actor, and Writer*

"I haven't read Bobby's book yet, but if it's anywhere near as good as his piano playing, or his stories, it's gonna be good."

– **Huey Lewis**
*Pop Superstar*

"From the first session Bobby Wood and I did together, I loved his playing. He could make a piano sing—literally. After that first session, Billy Sherrill used Bobby on every other session we did together. Not only is Bobby a great musician, he is a great friend."

– **George Jones**
*Country Music Legend*

"Bobby Wood and I have been great friends from the moment we first met in 1967. Our first meeting was at the American Studio in Memphis, Tennessee when Mark James called me in Houston and said that I should come to Memphis. He said that Chips Moman and the American Studio Group, were making hit records and he thought that we would be great together. So, I drove up and we tried some songs just as demos. The band and I fit together perfectly—from the first note we sounded like we had always been a band.

"Bobby always seemed to know exactly how each of the songs should go, and so did the rest of the guys. All of us became the best of friends right from the start. Chips told me that if I moved to Memphis, he could guarantee that we would cut hit records. So, I moved up with my brother Jerry and recorded 'The Eyes of a New York Woman,' by Mark James in one of the first sessions. 'New York Woman' led to 'Hooked on a Feeling,' which many consider to be my finest recording."

– **B.J. Thomas**
*Recording Artist*

"Bobby has been my treasured friend since we were kids in Memphis. His talents as a musician, songwriter, and singer have blessed my work as a producer from the very beginning—and have amazed me, always. It's hard to even imaging making music without him. NO ONE knows more about making a great record or has more fun with the process. As a man, as a musician, as a friend, he's as soulful and true as it gets.

"Hey, Bobby! Thank you for being here, pal."

– **Allen Reynolds**
*Producer and Songwriter*

"Bobby Wood is probably the best-kept secret in Memphis music. He is the most commercial sounding piano player to ever come out of Memphis. He's not only a player but also a writer, a great singer, and he's a really nice guy. Elvis loved his playing."

– **George Klein**
*Elvis Confidant and Memphis Disc Jockey*

"I met Bobby in 1962. He was playing some shows at the Millington Naval Base and hired me to play guitar in his band. Some time later, in the 1960's, after he got out of the Army, he came to work for me at American Studio in Memphis. His talent was a real asset and a vital part of all the music made at American.

"We are still in touch with each other after all these years and occasionally have the opportunity to make a little music together."

**– Chips Moman**
*Producer*

"This is the story of a man who has got music in his heart. Bobby, you are a great talent as a songwriter, a champion as a producer and a genius as a piano player. Your contributions to the history of modern music are outstanding. I deeply appreciate our friendship, I love your sense of humor and I wish you another 50 years of success and fun."

**– Peter Beines**
*Promoter and Former President of Elvis Fan Club—Germany*

"I have never known anyone like Bobby Wood. A best friend and virtuoso musician with a graceful, loving, generous, huge heart, he not only makes every recording session he plays on so much better, he elevates the spirit of everyone he encounters. Bobby's contribution to so many masterful song interpreters has transcended the ordinary and made each artist better. He's played with everyone from John Prine to Dusty Springfield; from the Wicked Wilson Pickett to Elvis Presley to Garth Brooks, and he's left his distinctive, stylistic mark on every track.

"Knowing and working with Bobby over the years has been one of the great pleasures of my life. Elvis certainly expressed his admiration by recording Bobby's great Memphis hit, 'If I'm A Fool For Loving You,' which was written by another Memphis [and Sun] legend, Stan Kesler. You can't beat Bobby—no one has even bothered to try—he's a true individual in every sense of both words, which over the years, I've come to recognize as one of the greatest accomplishments you can achieve in life. My dad once said that when Bobby Wood sits down at the piano, something spiritual is about to happen."

**– Knox Phillips**
*Record Producer*

"I have known Bobby Wood for over 40 years. He is one of my dearest friends. He has a feel on the piano that I love, and he has great ideas in the studio. I even got a chance to play on his recording of 'If I'm A Fool For Loving You.' I will never forget the friendship that Bobby and I have had throughout the years.

"Bobby is the kind of person that will stick with you in times of need. When I moved to Nashville, Bobby was the first to help me to get work and I will never forget that. He will also pray for whomever needs help in a hurry. He is the greatest.

"Love to my dearest friend."

**– Gene Chrisman (Bubba)**
*Member, The Memphis Boys*

"Bobby Wood is a true friend and surpasses all of the requirements for a true brother except for blood kin and sibling rivalry. I have many times been inspired to try as hard for me as he was trying for me. 'O brother where art thou' does not apply. He has been 'right there' with his offers of considerable help in everything he knew I was undertaking. After 51 years, I say whoever picked "the hardest working man in show business" never followed Bobby Wood for one day."

**– Bobby Emmons**
*Member, The Memphis Boys*

"Bobby and I have had a long musical journey together. We met in the early 60's back in Memphis, and I'm proud to say that he is one of my best friends. I admire his talent and creative ability as a musician and a songwriter, and I respect him as a Christian man who has a sincere love for Christ."

**– Reggie Young**
*Member, The Memphis Boys*

I've known Bobby Wood since the early 60's and we have watched each other grow in this crazy business called music. While that's true, it's just a small part of the lives we lead while on this 'trip.' Some artists have tagged Bobby the "Intro King." I've sat in the studio and watched and listened while Bobby created and invented some of the most fascinating intros. Bobby probably doesn't know this, but I have always listened in awe to his playing, not just intros but also the entire path he would create during the "crux" of the song.

"As I mentioned, music is but a small part of being a true, professional musician. During our over 40 years of working together and knowing each other, we've seen one another go through many "changes," apart from the actual requirements to become successful studio musicians. He's seen me at my very worst, and in other situations, my very best. The same goes for Bobby. In the studio, there are events that might occur that do not necessarily represent the job you were called in to perform. Bobby has dealt with these situations as best as he could, as we all would in our own way.

"While Bobby and I might not agree with each other about life and paths we may choose to take, I have never disagreed with him about music and the directions we would take with songs and arrangements. He may not know this, but I have always considered him to be the finest keyboard player I've ever worked with in the studio—or live. His sense of time/tempo is nothing short of incredible. He also has the ability to perform and create some of the best, most interesting melodic passages I've ever heard, while maintaining his impeccable sense of tempo.

"If this book reflects Bobby's life anywhere near the fine person I have know over the years, the reader needs to sit back and be ready for a fascinating adventure. His humor is unmatched and his spiritual life is enviable. I also consider him to be one of my dearest and best friends.

"To Bobby with all my love."

– **Mike Leech**
*Member, The Memphis Boys*

"Wilson Pickett's 'I'm In Love,' Neil Diamond's 'Sweet Caroline,' and Elvis Presley's 'Kentucky Rain.' I've been listening to Bobby Wood's piano playing since I was in high school. But it was years later, the first time I had the opportunity to play some music with him in the recording studio, that I realized what a solid, soulful, creative, and downright wonderful player he really is."

– **Chris Leuzinger**
*Musician, Member, The "G" Men*

"Many good musicians landed in Memphis during the 1950's and 1960's, but none were more talented than Bobby Wood—a great session player, singer, and songwriter with many hits to his credit."

– **Stanley Kesler**
*Record Producer and Writer*

"It has been my privilege to have been a small part of Bobby Wood's creative life for the last few decades. Among the many gifts that Bobby brings to the music business is 'taste.' 'Taste' is the most special and rarest commodity in our industry! As a musician, all you have to do is listen to the magic of the intro to Garth Brooks' 'The Dance,' or as a writer, listen to the heartbreak in the melody of Crystal Gayle's 'Talkin' In Your Sleep' to recognize his genius. The world of music is a much richer place because there is a Bobby Wood. Thank you, Bobby!"

– **Ralph Murphy**
*Writer and Publisher*

"I've known my pal, Woodburner, as long as I have been in the music business. I've watched him evolve from a beginning piano player, playing in pickup bands, to a guy trying to get on recording sessions in Memphis to a keyboard player everyone in the country is trying to get on their sessions. He's played for some of the biggest artists on the planet over the past century and is still going strong.

We've been very close for a long, long time. I'm so proud of his musical growth, but what makes me even happier for Bobby is his growth and great faith in our Lord Jesus Christ."

**– Dickey Lee**
*Recording Artist*

"Bobby Wood is a:
   Comic
   Jokester
   Piano playing son of a gun
   Session leader
   Piano playing son of a gun
   Songwriter
   Piano playing son of a gun
   Hit songwriter
   Piano playing son of a gun
   Great friend
   Piano playing son of a gun"

**– Jerry Phillips (son of Sam Phillips)**
*Sun Records*

"Bobby is one of a handful of musicians who have left their fingerprints on some of the most historic and popular recordings in most every genre of American music for over five decades."

**– Joe Chambers**
*Musicians Hall of Fame and Museum*

"Bobby Wood is the original soul man. The only thing bigger than his talent is his heart. Bobby knows as much about making hit records as anyone in the world. I'm a lucky engineer to have witnessed Bobby Wood's talent throughout my career. He not only makes sessions fun, he makes them right. Love you, pal."

**– Mark Miller**
*Studio Engineer*

"You know Bobby Wood through his music. He has contributed his talent to hundreds of pop, country, and soul hits and was chosen in the first class inducted into the Musician's Hall of Fame.

"Truly, his music has touched all of our souls. I've known Bobby for the last thirty-five years and have heard all these hits and a lot more. I feel blessed because of that alone, but his friendship has blessed me even more. Bobby is truly one of the kindest people I have ever known—a man who is always there to lend a hand to those in need. He's a very giving person, a man who gives us his wonderful music and his precious time.

"Now he is giving us his intriguing life story. It's a tale taking us behind the scenes of the soundtrack to the last fifty years."

– **Anita Hogin**
Music Management

"I had known the talent of Bobby Wood for many years in the recording studios in Nashville, but the day I began to love Bobby was in Johannesburg, South Africa, while sitting outside on the hotel lawn. My husband, Pete Drake, was producing an album on the top ten country acts in South Africa. Pete had asked Bobby to be one of the studio musicians for the recording sessions. After an exhausting trip (long days and many hours in the studio with new artists that were not familiar with the way musicians recorded in Nashville) Pete turned to Bobby and said, 'Something about you is different; what's happened to you?'

"Bobby just smiled and said, 'I don't need any of that other stuff any more. I found Jesus.'

"I remember Pete saying to me, after watching Bobby for the duration of the trip, 'I don't know what has happened to Bobby but I want some of it.'

"That trip with Bobby Wood changed Pete's life. He came back to Nashville, found Bobby's church, became a Christian and lived the rest of his life for Christ. Bobby never said one word to Pete *about the changes he had made in his life—he just lived it so Pete could see it.*

*"God bless you, Bobby Wood."*

**– Rose Drake**
*Wife of the late Pete Drake - Producer and Session Musician*

# *Prologue*

Sonley Roush was driving the car that carried Bobby Wood and other band members to their next concert. It was early morning hours and the destination was not that far. It was, however, far enough and he felt the fatigue set in on his body. Yet, he was so close to Lima that he decided to push on to the end of the destination. He had been weaving on and off the road for some time.

Suddenly, there was a swerve that was too sudden and the driver was traveling too fast. A semi-truck was in the oncoming traffic from the opposite direction. Just before dawn on October 23, 1964, the car that was carrying the band members hit the semi-truck head on at a speed of approximately fifty miles per hour.

Seat belts were not installed in cars during those days.

Bobby Wood went through the front windshield of the car. His shoulders kept him from going all the way through the glass, but he was caught in the glass of the windshield. Bobby's face caught the brunt of the injuries, as it was stuck in the glass. One of the band members literally had to pull the door off the car because it was jammed. Then they proceeded to pull Bobby out of the windshield. The entire right side of his face was virtually destroyed. He lost his right eye.

Sonley Roush, the driver of the car, died within a few minutes of the accident.

Bobby was rushed to a hospital in Lima, Ohio. The paramedics later said that Bobby was answering questions as well as giving phone numbers, but he imself had no recollection of that. Then, Bobby went from sleep to shock in an instant.

What would this life-altering event do to Bobby Wood? Could he still find his place in the music world? Would he ever again realize his dream?

- **Barbara Wood Lowry**

# *Chapter One*

### The Early Years

Bobby Wood was always destined to have a career in music. In fact, with his family it was never a question. Bobby was born in the tiny community of Mitchell Switch, Mississippi, which is just south of New Albany, Mississippi, in Union County and is no more than a wide place in the road. There was a train track where the train would switch tracks, thus the name. If anyone thought that they would never hear of this place in rural Mississippi, then they just hadn't thought that a talent like Bobby Wood could come from a "wide place in the road."

Bobby's music heritage began with his grandparents, Walter and Kittie Cox Wood. Walter and Kittie had eleven children. One child died as an infant, leaving ten children for Walter and Kittie to raise. Farming was their way of life and their main source of income. The Wood family raised cows so they could sell the milk, as well as pigs. They grew vegetables, corn, and hay and sold about ten bales of cotton per year.

But Walter waited for those times when he could sing. All

ten of the children were taught music before they learned to read a Primer. They were taught to sing the old-fashioned do-re-mi form of music as soon as they learned how to talk.

Walter had been trained by Professor J.H. Stanley at the Stanley Music School in Saltillo, Mississippi, as well as with a well-known music teacher by the name of R.N. Grishom. At one point, Walter had even trained in French opera. Some of his music education was by mail order catalog, but he would learn the music and do whatever it took to make it sound right.

Having quickly determined that his love was gospel music, Walter graduated from the Bond Music Company with a music certification. With that certification, he led music for revivals. At one point he decided that everyone should have the opportunity to learn music. After all, who wouldn't want to be able to sing?

In the late 1800's and early 1900's the only means of communication was by word of mouth or by mail. Knowing that, Walter Wood sat down and wrote letters to surrounding churches about starting a singing school. He outlined what he would offer and told of the joys of learning music. Coley Chapel, located on the east side of Union County, responded favorably.

Walter set up his school, and for the first class there were one hundred and twenty-five students in attendance. Each person paid three dollars for attending the three-week school, however some did not have three dollars to pay, so they paid with groceries, bushels of vegetables, or whatever they could bring from the garden.

People would load up in their wagons and travel to Coley Chapel for Walter Wood's singing school. They were taught music from the *Vaughn* or *Baxter Music Book*, which contained basic note music as well as some hymns. Walter loved the old hymns that were slow songs. He wanted to hear the words.

With a music book in one hand and his melodious bass voice, Walter taught his students to sing. Once they accomplished the singing parts, every student was required to direct. Walter thought that if you could sing then you should be able to lead a group of people in congregational singing.

One of Walter's last opportunities to direct was in 1961, just months before he died. He was taken by some of his family members to a singing convention. Word quickly traveled through the crowd that Walter Wood was in the audience. Once his presence was known, Walter was brought up on the stage. The emcee asked him if he would like to direct. In his weak, feeble voice, he immediately said, "yes." He was then asked if he wanted his son, Leslie, to help him. He was quick to say that no help was needed.

He gingerly leaned over to the emcee and added, "If I need help, I'll ask for it."

Shakily, Walter Edward Wood stood up and began to lead the congregation in one last song.

When he was finished, there was not one dry eye in the house. Many of those in attendance had been his students. All knew of his musical abilities. Walter Wood was singing his farewell. But with that farewell (it was not known then) his heritage would live on—especially through one very talented grandson.

All of the Wood children went to this singing school. Attendance was not an option. Singing was as important as eating or doing chores. At one point in time, some of the kids were a part of a string band, which consisted of a mandolin, guitars, banjos, and fiddles. Gospel music was the music of the soul. Gospel quartets were very popular in those days, and the Wood children were all introduced to this genre of music. You might say that Walter was a gospel music "junkie" and his kids had no choice but to follow suit.

Born on August 8, 1905, Leslie Herman "Pap" Wood was the second of Walter and Kittie's children. He was no different than any of the other Wood children. He learned to sing.

Leslie used to take a little pump organ to the school and would play it while his father taught his singing class at the church, for as long as a week at a time. Often, Walter and Leslie would stay overnight with different families during the week. Their mode of travel during those days was horse and buggy, making long-distance travel difficult.

Walter made sure that his children embraced music and tried to impart his passion of music to all of them. Their second child, Leslie, seemed a natural for this same talent and love of music, which he displayed even as a young child.

In 1924 Leslie Wood married Eunie Pickens. They met at church and were married by the local minister. Leslie and Eunie had seven children. Maxine was the first-born. After Maxine, there was Irene, Etoye, Robert Edward, Billy, Bobby, and Jamie.

Leslie and Eunie brought their first four children into this world and surrounded them with love and music. One Sunday after church, other close family members joined Leslie, Eunie, and their four children for lunch. As they all enjoyed lunch around the table, Eunie gave Robert Edward some English peas that she had gathered from the garden. But something was wrong, very wrong. In just a matter of hours Robert Edward developed colic. In those days, doctors were not nearby and did not really know how to treat colic, so Robert Edward Wood died at the age of eighteen months.

Eunie carried the burden of the death of her first-born son for the rest of her life. She suffered from depression over the loss of her beloved son. However, with three children in tow and three more that were born over the next few years, Eunie marched through life with her faith and the strength of her family.

Those remaining four girls and two boys were taught the same music principles that Walter had taught his children. The Wood children were not given a choice—when it was time to practice music, everything else stopped.

Life was simple in those days. Leslie and Eunie were not rich by any stretch of the imagination, but they never considered themselves poor. Just like their parents, Leslie and Eunie farmed. Education was a luxury. Leslie went through the ninth grade because that was the last grade taught at his school, and Eunie went through the eighth grade for the same reason. In the early 1900's, farming was one of the few things that people knew how to do, especially in the deep south. When you finished your level of education, you helped support your family through farming or whatever the family business was at the time.

This timeframe was between the Great Depression and World War II. Government programs were available for farmers. The banks were lenient with the local farmers, and, for those who didn't have the money to pay their loans, the banks would allow delay of payment until the following year.

Leslie and Eunie wanted to have their own farm to raise their family, but it would be a while before that could happen. Leslie was a hard worker. He and Eunie, along with their children, lived just outside of New Albany on a piece of property near New Harmony where Leslie worked as a sharecropper until he could buy his own land.

Even though Leslie only had a ninth grade education, he was always good at business decisions. The surrounding area was ninety percent farmland. Sharecropping wasn't in the plan, but Leslie knew what he had to do to ensure that the farm supported his family.

The time finally came that Leslie and Eunie could buy a home for their family. They bought a one hundred acre farm south of New Albany. The old home place, as they liked to call it, had a wooded area, a big lake, a big two-story home, a barn, and an outbuilding. In fact, the outbuilding, or outhouse as it was called, was a small structure. There were Sears catalogs hanging on wires which were used for toilet paper. The water was hand-pumped. Eunie would heat some water and pour it into a zinc tub with some cold water, and then all of the children would take a bath. There was also a smoke house that was used for hanging or storing meat. Oil lamps were used for lighting. In 1940, Leslie had paid $7,000 for the entire piece of land and the buildings on it. The one hundred acres were mostly used for cultivation.

Life was very simple—no frills.

Bobby Ray Wood was born on January 25, 1941. The world was in turmoil during this time, as World War II was still a part of the global scene. In fact, just eleven months after Bobby's birth, the world experienced the bombing of Pearl Harbor. Certain foods and supplies were rationed. While Leslie did not like standing in the ration lines, he did what he had to do to receive some of the basics—the things that they did not grow or raise. He always made sure that his family had the basic necessities of life.

Bobby has early remembrances of living on the farm. The family had been in their home in the Mitchell Switch community about three years. This was the first home that the Wood family had purchased.

In 1944, when Bobby was three years old, the old home place burned. Leslie had taken the family to Tupelo for the day, and they returned home just after dark. Leslie brought in a gallon can of gasoline to start a fire in the cook stove so Eunie could prepare supper but did not realize that the coals were still hot from breakfast. When the gasoline hit the coals, the heat was so intense that the can exploded in his hand and Leslie found himself burning—he was on fire. Fire immediately engulfed the kitchen and it was ablaze.

Leslie ran outside and began to roll in a mud puddle to extinguish the fire from his burning body. Fortunately, the burns on Leslie's body were moderate, most likely because it had just rained and the mud was wet and soft. Eunie grabbed the children and ran outside of the burning home. Standing outside, huddled with their children, all Leslie and Eunie could do was watch their home go up in flames. In a matter of minutes, the house and all of their belongings were nothing but ashes.

The only things that the Wood family had were the clothes on their backs. But, being small town, USA, this community pulled together. In a short amount of time, someone offered an empty house rent-free. Word of this tragedy quickly spread throughout the community. Neighbors and churches pulled together and received donations to replace food, clothes, and furniture. Of course, there was no insurance, but there was a large wooded area on the property. Leslie was able to sell enough lumber to build another house.

With another house built, life continued as it had been. Bobby was eight years old before the family got any type of electricity. He remembers that at the age of ten the family also got indoor plumbing. Leslie installed the plumbing himself.

The first night after the bath was installed Eunie went into the bathroom and closed the door. The children could hear the water running. Some time after the water stopped running, there was no noise coming from the bathroom. The kids were all concerned and wondered what was happening, so one of Bobby's sisters went to check on her mom. She came out of the bathroom in tears because she was laughing so hard. Eunie was sitting on the side of the tub with her feet in the water.

Her daughter looked at her and said, "Mama, you are supposed to get in the tub."

Eunie replied, "Do you think that I am going to wash my face with the same water that I am sitting in?"

Leslie never allowed Eunie to work in the cotton fields or do the chores like milking cows or feeding the animals. He always figured that she bore seven children, and her hands were full with doing all of the cooking, cleaning, and taking care of the family.

Eunie was an excellent cook. She was taught by her mother

and never used a recipe. She would just take a pinch of this and a pinch of that and made the best food anyone would ever want to taste. She could put together a three-course meal and have it on the table quicker than anyone in Union County. She made perfect biscuits, cooked vegetables grown from her own garden, and fried chicken that was unmatched by anyone. Her pies and cakes were award-winning, but she cooked for her family. She knew what they liked. When the meals were finished, she would put a plate over each of the bowls and anyone who came for a visit, whether a friend or a stranger, would be expected to sit down and eat. That's when the plates would come off the top of the bowls and the food would be served.

One of the things Eunie invented for her own family was chocolate syrup. Sometimes that would be served to the family as an extra treat. The children would butter the hot biscuits and pour the rich chocolate syrup over the biscuits. Those were special days and there was always plenty. Then while everyone ate, Eunie would entertain with stories of her past. She always brought a smile and laugh to those around her.

One of Bobby's chores around the house was the churning. Of course, to a young boy, churning was extremely monotonous. Bobby had to wait for the milk in the churn to clabber, and then it had to be churned. The butter would eventually rise to the top. Eunie would collect the butter and put it into the butter molds. Needless to say, Bobby could not wait for his churning chore to end.

While the Wood family continued to farm, Leslie continued to teach his children to sing just as his father had taught him. While Walter, Leslie's father, loved the slow hymns, Leslie was developing a love for the faster paced music. Walter once told Leslie that the fast music was "music for the foot, not the heart." This did not discourage Leslie nor change his course. He began to teach his children the music from the Quartet Conventions, especially groups like the Blackwood Brothers.

Leslie would stand Bobby and his little sister, Jamie, on the piano bench, and, even at a very young age, all of the Wood children would sing those old-time, favorite gospel songs. Each of the children learned to sing harmony by ear. They had no sheet music; they just had lyrics written on a piece of paper.

At one time, Bobby took a music correspondence course from Leroy Abernathy, a funky piano player who had developed his own style. Bobby was about eight years old when this course was offered. He took a few lessons and became quite disinterested. By then he was already picking up rhythms on his own. He already had an ear for music. To this day, Bobby cannot read music. He will tell you that he "just hears the music in his head and plays by ear." The Wood kids learned chords from the song. Their parts were chosen based on the range of their voice. Usually, Bobby would sing lead, Jamie would sing tenor, and Etoye would sing baritone.

While playing outside one day, Bobby was with his brother and sisters as well as some other children. There were tire swings, tree limb ponies, basketball goal and other imaginative yard "toys." Leslie called for the children to come in and practice, but Bobby had other ideas. He was having too much fun in the yard. Leslie came outside and gave Bobby a swat and told him it was time to practice his music. With tears rolling down his face, Bobby was told to "SING," and "SING" is what he did. When it was time to practice, the kids would stand around the old piano in the front room, Leslie would light the oil lamps and the kids practiced singing gospel music. Billy was the one child who did not really want to sing, so he played the guitar. That's just the way things were back then. There were no questions.

Leslie was a farmer just like his father. He loved farming and that is how the family provided for themselves. But just like his father Walter, Leslie's passion was music.

Leslie was a gospel music disc jockey for a local radio station. He made friends with a man who opened up a radio station in New Albany. Leslie Wood and Charlie Boren did a phone patch for a remote broadcast by phone line from New Albany. Leslie "Pap" Wood hosted the *Pap Wood's Gospel Radio Hour* and the *Singing Convention of the Air*. Leslie was not only the disc jockey, but he also did local advertising on the radio.

The Wood children sang the first song for the opening of WELO radio station. They sang "Turn Your Radio On." Listeners heard this unique family talent. Correspondence was handled through the mail since there were no phones out in the country. People soon began to write Pap Wood at the radio station, asking for the family to give a concert.

Because of his connections and contacts, the Wood family traveled throughout Mississippi, Alabama, Tennessee, and sometimes Arkansas to singing conventions. Gas, motel, and food expenses were usually covered, but the real honor was being on stage with the quartet legends that performed after them. The Wood family would often be the opening group for concerts that included the Blackwood Brothers and the Statesmen Quartet. These groups were their heroes. Bobby's hero was Jake Hess; he copied Jake as often as he could. Later, Bobby found out that Jake was also Elvis Presley's quartet icon. Singing with these groups brought incredible excitement to the Wood family.

That went on for many years. In some cases, Pap would schedule a concert and ask to use the high school auditorium. Admission was usually one dollar. When named quartets would appear, the quartet would get the money and the Wood family got the exposure. One perk was that meals were usually provided at these singing conventions. Those were the days of "dinner on the grounds," consisting of fried chicken, banana pudding, home grown vegetables, and all of the extra trimmings. No one ever went away hungry. Times were still tight, and a good meal was good pay.

Getting to those concerts or conventions was not always easy. At one point, the county paid Leslie as a school bus driver. With six children traveling to these concerts, Leslie decided that going by school bus was an economical and roomy way to take a trip, so he had someone make him a school bus out of tin. The top had a shingle roof on it. It actually looked like a house going down the road. Interestingly, the county allowed Leslie to drive his homemade bus and added it to their fleet of school buses.

The kids did not particularly care for this "singing school bus." In fact, Bobby was so embarrassed to go "anywhere in a thing like that." Leslie called it his singing school bus, but the kids called it their nightmare. On occasion, the family would go to the big singing convention in Booneville or Baldwin, Mississippi, in this "traveling house." Bobby has memories of being so embarrassed that he would wait until everybody else had gone inside before he would get out of the bus so that no one would see him.

Once, during a singing convention in Booneville, the Wood family drove up in this traveling nightmare. Just as they entered the parking lot, the Goodman family, a well-known quartet, drove up in their big black Cadillac. All Bobby could think is, "Where can I hide?"

Of course nobody made a lot of money back then. Besides the land, they had their home, a chicken house, outbuildings, and smoke house. They had eighty acres in cotton that they raised. They also had some corn; a few milk cows, pigs, chickens, and a couple mules. Not only that, they had fifteen acres of wooded area and a lake. Leslie built a storm cellar that was located on a bank off the road, but later he built a concrete storm cellar behind the house. He wanted to ensure that his family was safe in case of tornadoes, since the community was at the edge of a tornado path that basically destroyed Tupelo.

School started in early summer but let out in late September for two weeks so that the farming families could gather their crops. All of this had to happen to provide food and income, but the singing continued. Practice was still put into the daily family schedule.

In those days they farmed with mules and all of the kids had to help with planting the cotton and corn. Since there was no machinery available, everything had to be done by hand. The harvest had to be gathered within that two weeks so that the kids could return to school. Everyone had to pull his or her own load to make this happen. The mules were used when planting the cotton, but when it came time to thin it out, everyone had to use a hoe. The acres used for the cotton had to be planted and cultivated.

Bobby started playing the piano when he was about nine years old. His brother, Billy, had gotten a Sears and Roebuck guitar for Christmas one year. It was a Silvertone and had one very small amp. Bobby started to try to play it, but the strings were so far off the neck it would just cut his fingers raw. Because it seemed to be so painful learning to play the guitar, Bobby decided that he would learn to play the piano instead. The family had an old upright piano that his dad and sisters had played. Since he did not know any melodies, Bobby started playing rhythm on the old piano. He learned a three-fingered rhythm and played the left hand notes just one at a time with one finger.

"I can remember being in the first or second grade and kids would pay pennies, nickels, and dimes for me to sing for them," said Bobby.

And he would sing.

"When I was around six or seven years old, we went to Memphis to what was then the Ellis Auditorium to sing for the weekend gospel convention," Wood said.

Leslie was always the spokesperson for the group. He did the talking and scheduled all of the bookings. He took the kids to all of the different churches in the area to sing. One year the Wood family entered a local talent show. As might be expected, they sang their gospel songs and they were overwhelmingly chosen as the winner. This win took them to the next level of competition, where again they were the winners. This path continued all the way to the finals, which were held at Ellis Auditorium in Memphis, Tennessee. The Wood family came out as victors and won the grand prize, which was a paid trip to perform on stage at the Grand Ole Opry.

With this honor, the Wood family continued to perform around the mid-south. There was name recognition. People knew who they were and were anxious to see this talented family on stage.

On occasion there would be friends that would join in with the family to play or sing. One acquaintance, Mrs. Scott, would come and play the piano. Her daughters, Peggy and Jimmie Dale, would sometimes sing as well.

On one particular Saturday the Wood family was at the radio station performing on Leslie's show. Bobby was almost eleven years old at that time. Peggy pulled a picture out of her wallet to show Bobby.

She looked at him and said, "I want you to look at the picture of this guy. He is really going to be famous one day. He is from Tupelo, Mississippi and he is recording for Sun Records. His name is Elvis Presley. I have seen him perform and he is really good."

That was Bobby's first introduction to Elvis Presley. Bobby knew that Tupelo was just about twenty miles down the road, but he hadn't heard the name until that very moment. It wouldn't be the last time he heard it either. He filed the name in his memory and it would prove to be a name that would be etched into music history, and become a part of Bobby's life—beyond even his wildest dreams.

Once again the family traveled back to Memphis for another weekend convention. Doris Shields was a family friend who had played the piano for the Wood family on previous visits. She was a fan and thought the Wood kids had tremendous talent. She suggested to Leslie that he should meet a friend of hers who owned a recording studio. Doris Shields' friend just happened to be Sam Phillips at Sun Studio. Of course, Leslie and his children had no knowledge of the significance of being taken to such an historic recording studio.

So, on Saturday afternoon before the singing, Leslie and his children went to the Sun Records studio and recorded some of their favorite gospel songs. They booked the studio for two hours and paid twenty dollars.

Bobby said, "I remember that we sang 'This Old House.' It was one of the more popular gospel songs and we loved to sing it."

They also sang "Heavenly Love," another popular gospel song of that day. There were some other songs but these were among the favorites. Sam Phillips had a million dollar personality, and he gave a lot of encouragement to Etoye, Jamie, and Bobby as they sang. He told the youngsters how much he enjoyed their singing. Although they just did the one session, they felt like they had just reached a real milestone in making their first recording.

After the family had finished recording, they were in the front lobby of the studio talking with Sam. Bobby noticed a picture of Elvis Presley underneath the glass on the front desk of the studio. Immediately, he told Sam about Peggy and her picture. What Bobby did not realize is that Elvis was sitting behind the desk. In fact, he did not even recognize him because Elvis did not look anything like his picture. Bobby remembers that Elvis was not clean-shaven, his hair was not dark, and his features were much different than the picture, so it was easy to see why Bobby did not know who he was.

After a few minutes of conversation, Sam Phillips looked at

Bobby and said, "Meet Elvis Presley."

Bobby shook hands with Elvis but was so embarrassed that he did not know him. In true Elvis fashion, he shook hands with Bobby and told him that he loved gospel music. He also complimented Bobby and his family, telling them that they had a good sound. Bobby could not contain his excitement.

Elvis had just released "That's Alright Mama," and his career was about to explode. As a ten-year-old kid, Bobby had no idea that he would cross paths with Elvis many years later, but for a much different reason.

## Chapter Two

FROM GOSPEL TO ROCK AND ROLL

When Bobby was about 15 years old and still in school, he started a rock and roll band aptly titled the Bobby Wood Band. The band consisted of Bobby Wood who played piano, Ronald Young on the drums, Joe Young played bass, and Sammy Allen played guitar. The band was the rage of the school. Teachers and students alike loved to hear the band perform. Many times they were asked to perform for the chapel program on Wednesday mornings.

All of the band members had the same passion for music and they all loved to perform. Every Sunday they would meet at Bobby's house to rehearse, but during the week they rehearsed at the radio station. During those Sunday rehearsals, you could count on Leslie, Bobby's father, to walk through with his usual assessment of their music, "Ya'll shouldn't be playing that music." But the folks in the area, especially the teenagers, had a very different opinion.

Word traveled quickly throughout the community. The

Bobby Wood Band was creating a music frenzy in Union County, Mississippi. Soon the radio station jumped on board and at 12:30 on Saturday afternoon everyone tuned in to hear the music group. Of course, this was right before Pap Wood's radio program at 1:00 pm that same afternoon.

There were five county schools in the surrounding area. As word traveled, all of the schools were jumping on the bandwagon and booked Bobby's band for school events. The only school that seemed to have a problem with the music was Bobby's school—Ingomar High School. The principal did not like or have any appreciation for the style of music that the band played. They were strictly rock and roll and like so many in the church community, the principal agreed with local preachers, that they performed the "devil's music."

But as luck would have it, the teacher who taught typing and bookkeeping was also responsible for the school play. She needed someone to entertain for intermission during the play performance, so she asked Bobby and his group. They had fifteen minutes and were to play four songs. Jerry Lee Lewis had hit the music scene and Bobby had learned to play just like him, so what better song to arouse a crowd than 'Great Balls of Fire!' The principal was furious. He immediately turned off the lights so that the students could not see the band. This, however, was not a showstopper. The band continued to play and the students went wild. Even in the dark, the enthusiasm could not be curtailed.

Bobby heard Jerry Lee's release of 'Crazy Arms' and 'You Win Again,' and after that, he was hooked. Bobby bought these records and taught himself how to play them note for note. Once Bobby learned those songs he would get more records and would learn to play them, note by note. He learned the Jerry Lee Lewis style of playing and built his original style around that of the "Killer."

Bobby continued to sing with his family, but his show that preceded the family show was drawing a lot of attention. Bobby wanted to have that "right sound" for his band. Sammy Allen had left for college, so in order to have the sound that was needed on the radio; Bobby hired a guitar player by the name of Elbert Adair. Elbert played a lot like James Burton who backed up Ricky Nelson on the Ozzie and Harriett Show. This guy had picked up that style that Bobby Wood had become accustomed to hearing. Along with Elbert Adair, Joe Wilson, and Ronald Young, the band had a great sound.

The more Bobby played, the more he developed a style that would emulate Jerry Lee Lewis. That was his connection to rock and roll, and whether he played gospel or rock and roll, he played with that unique sound and flair. He continued to play for a couple of local quartets as well as playing for the family on the Saturday radio show.

The Bobby Wood Band went to a local fair and competed. They won the first day in their elimination round, but on the second day they lost to an opera singer, so they came home.

With his band in tact, Bobby went to the state finals of the Future Farmers of America Band Contest. There were several preliminaries, but Bobby and his band ended up at the finals playing the Jerry Lee Lewis music. They placed second in the Mississippi finals. A guy named Bobby Emmons led the group that ended up winning first place. Emmons played the piano and they had a guy that impersonated Elvis pretty well. While Wood and his group did Jerry Lee, Emmons and his group did Elvis.

Many years later, Wood and Emmons would again be together as a part of the American Studio Band and the Memphis Boys.

Bobby's parents were not too happy about him switching from gospel to rock and roll. Bobby knew what he loved to play but could feel the pull from his family to stay with the gospel music. However, during all of the disagreements over the direction that Bobby should take with his music, his father never told him that he could not play rock and roll.

The Bobby Wood Band made a name for themselves. At one point the band went to Memphis to cut a record. They started with a recording company with the most known name at the time—Sun Records. Sun said no, but during those days, there was a recording company on every corner in mid-town Memphis. After many calls, the band found a record company who would let them put down their songs—OJAY Records.

The first song the band recorded, 'Love Is My Business,' was written by Quinton Claunch. The second song, 'Kiss Me Quick,' was written by Steppin' Fetchit and needed a saxophone player. They found one in Freddie Boy Burns, a blind player who played with Slim Rhodes on WMC Radio every day.

During the forties and fifties, southern preachers were often called "hell, fire, and brimstone" preachers. There was more emphasis on what was wrong and less on the love of God. Most of the area churches held the same beliefs. On one particular Sunday, girls were told that if they went to prom they would go to hell. They were asked to bring their prom dresses to the church where they would be destroyed. The messages from the pulpit condemned everything from television to comic books to music. Many preachers called the songs from Elvis Presley and Jerry Lee Lewis the devil's music.

Pressure began to build from the pulpit and from the adults in the church. The young people who played or listened to rock and roll were being ostracized. There were entire sermons preached on the evil doings of Elvis and Jerry Lee. Sunday after Sunday, Bobby would hear sermons on the things that would send you to hell. Bobby did not agree with the preachers but felt an insurmountable pressure to "do something."

At one point Bobby felt caught up in the moment. Finally, he reached a point where he felt the need to walk the aisle of the church and rededicate his life to God. He wanted to play his music but he wanted to know and feel the love of God in his life.

This proved to be a life-changing moment.

At the time that Bobby walked to the front of the church to rededicate his life, the preacher turned to the entire congregation, and with Bobby at his side said, "Are you going to renounce rock and roll? You either renounce rock and roll or go to hell!"

As Bobby looked around, he felt a tremendous amount of pressure. The piano was playing. The congregation of approximately one hundred people had all eyes looking at him to see what he was going to do. Bobby could only feel humiliation and embarrassment at that time. He knew that if he said he would renounce rock and roll, then he would not only regret his answer, but he would be giving an answer that he could not live up to for a lifetime. If he said no, he was basically saying that he knew he would "go to hell" for his decision.

As a teenager and without guidance from anyone, he said that he would renounce rock and roll. The preacher had accomplished what he set out to do. All Bobby wanted to do was go home and be in the security of his family.

Once church was over, Bobby got alone with his father and asked him about the church incident. Leslie agreed with Bobby that the preacher should not have taken the approach that he used. Once again, Leslie never told Bobby that he could not play rock and roll. Although he did not agree with the music choice, he still allowed it to be Bobby's choice.

It was then that Bobby knew he would play rock and roll music. He did not feel that this was a sin and knew that it was his passion. He even remembers thinking, "If that is the case, if the preacher is right, then it's off to hell I go," because he knew he had to follow his heart for the music that he truly loved. But he also knew that he was a Christian and was heaven bound. He did not agree with the preacher's interpretation of his career choice.

The ridicule continued.

Bobby had a high school government teacher that was also the basketball coach. This coach had the best winning record in the mid-south and was sought after by high schools and colleges throughout the region. This coaching great had built an impeccable record in a small county Mississippi school. To this day the hallway is still filled with gold basketball trophies from winning state championships.

Bobby wasn't much of a basketball player. It's just something that the boys in the school did as a sports outlet. At that time Bobby weighed only ninety-nine pounds. But the coach put everything he had into being a winning team and having a winning attitude.

Even though this teacher put his focus on basketball, he also taught a government class. One day during class he asked the students to complete a budget sheet. They had to show where they were going to work after high school and how much money they planned to make. Most of the kids were planning on working at the local Futoria Furniture Factory and their budget was $40 to $50 per week.

Bobby knew that he was not going to stay in New Albany. His plan was to play music professionally or go to Hollywood and become an actor. Bobby completed his budget sheet and put down his career goals, listing his budget at $1000 per week. The teacher was furious with Bobby because he felt that he was not taking the assignment seriously, that he should have put down a more realistic budget.

The teacher turned to the class and said, "Wood, you will never amount to two cents."

At that point, you could have heard a pin drop. It was obvious that the other kids in the class felt bad for Bobby.

Again, Bobby sought the advice of his father. Leslie gave Bobby some of the most valuable counsel that he can remember. Not only did Leslie tell Bobby to rise above the comments, he also told him,

"You are no better than anyone else and no one else is any better than you. You have to be the best that you can be."

For Bobby, more determination just set in his mind and heart. He was determined to prove the teacher wrong. Public humiliation and negative statements were not drivers of decisions. They were forces that made Bobby more determined than ever to achieve his goals.

As he grew, Bobby recognized that those basketball principles were important in his life. That coach had taught him what it meant to be a winner. He taught him that you had to take that winning attitude and move in any direction that you would choose for your life.

While Bobby was frustrated and embarrassed with that initial response, as an adult he realized the importance of the words spoken by his coach. Many years later Bobby had the opportunity to shake his coach's hand and tell him that he loved and respected him.

The older kids had left home, leaving just Billy, Bobby, and Jamie. The two boys had continued to work the field. One year, it was time for the cotton to be picked. But illness had come upon the Wood family—they all had the flu. It didn't take long for word to spread throughout the church and the community.

On the following Monday morning the family awoke to the tune of trucks, cars, tractors and wagons. They were lined up in the driveway and still more on the road in front of their home. Dozens of people filed by the house and went straight to the cotton field. By noon the entire eighty plus acres of cotton had been picked. The tractors and wagons were filing back by the house on their way to the cotton gin.

While the outside work was being done by some of the neighbors, others began to come through the back door with armloads of cotton samples that were ready to be taken to town and sold. Leslie was so overcome with emotion that he began to cry. He didn't know how to say thank you in an appropriate manner so he began to hug everyone who came through the door. Bobby remembers that this is just one of a few times that he had ever seen his father cry. Once again, a small community gathered around and shared their love, time and talents with this very special family.

One of the major achievements associated with graduating from high school was the gift of five acres from Leslie to each of his two sons. When Billy, Bobby's older brother, was a senior in high school, Leslie gave him the back five acres of the cotton to cultivate. That would be his start in the family farming business. Leslie was going to give Billy the money that they made from cultivating the cotton so that Billy could get himself a car and so he did. Billy sold the crop from his five acres and made enough money to buy a Rocket '88 Oldsmobile.

Six years later, when Bobby graduated, Leslie offered Bobby the same thing. Bobby planted the land, cultivated it, and took care of it. However, that was a particularly bad year. Leslie needed the money from Bobby's crop to pay the bills.

Bobby and Leslie were on the tractor traveling to the cotton gin when he broke the news to Bobby that there would be no money from Bobby's crop. That money was for family survival and basic family needs. This broke Bobby's heart. He was hurt, angry, disappointed, and not old enough to understand how one brother could receive such a gift and the other could not.

In those days, you were expected "to look at things like a man." There was no discussion. There was no further explanation. It's just the way things were. Bobby did not see the disappointment from his father, who truly wanted to give Bobby the same gift that he had given Billy. Even though Bobby never received the crop money, things did improve. And later, Leslie helped Bobby get his first car—a 1954 Ford.

Times were hard and the family was very poor. They had to

have a roof over their heads and food to eat; the only purchases made at the store were for things like flour, sugar, salt, and other necessary staples. All of the other food was raised on the farm. There was a garden—a truck patch. Eunie canned in fruit jars.

Bobby remembers a time when his dad seemed particularly troubled. This time of concern went on for quite a while. Bobby later found out that because of a bad cotton year, there was not enough money to pay a bank note that was due. The bank was threatening to take the farm. Leslie was overcome with grief and worry. He went out behind the house under the big oak tree, fell to his knees and asked the Lord what he should do.

The Lord guided him.

The next day Leslie went to town to talk to the banker. A couple of hours later he came through the front door with a huge smile on his face. Instead of going to the bank where the loan was due, he went to the bank across the street. Since New Albany was a two-street town, there were only two banks.

The banker told Leslie that he would take over the loan and nothing would be owed until the next year when the crops came in. The Wood family had just experienced yet another miracle in their lives.

The times continued to be difficult. Another hard year came along and the money from the crops was needed to provide for the family.

Bobby was not particularly proud of the clothes he had to wear. Many of his shirts were made out of flour sacks. In those days, flour sacks came printed. There was no hiding what you were actually wearing, but Eunie would take the flour sacks and make shirts on her sewing machine.

Over time, these things gripped Bobby's thoughts. He felt that life had choices. He chose to build a life and career around the passion that his father taught him—his love for music. He chose to ignore the discouraging remarks by those that had influence in his life—his teachers, friends, and sometimes even his own family.

Bobby's Aunt Merdell was a beautician. Bobby's hair was already pretty blonde, but Bobby had her make it more blonde and put a permanent wave in it so that it would look more like Jerry Lee Lewis. Bobby's senior picture in the class annual was listed as "Bobby (Jerry Lee) Wood." The annual staff did this for Bobby. The kids all liked Bobby and they all liked Jerry Lee. What better way to remember the kid from Ingomar who brought music and soul to the school!

Throughout high school Bobby had talked to people like Stan Kesler, C.D. Smith, and his brother, Billy. Bobby met Stan through his brother, Billy. He knew that Stan was in the music business but didn't know what he did. C.D. was a family friend from Memphis who played bass with Johnny Burnett. Bobby had made known his desire to move to Memphis and record music. He wanted to meet those who were in the music business who might be able to help him in his own career.

When Bobby finished his formal education at Ingomar High School, he was still playing for a gospel quartet group—one that he had been with for about eight months. Bobby knew that his calling was not with the quartet music, so after a lot of thought, he told the quartet members that he was going to Memphis to pursue a music career and gave his notice that he was leaving the group. One member of the group looked at him and with that same sternness that Bobby had heard before, Mr. McKinney said, "You need to stay away from that rock and roll; you are never going to be good enough to do anything with that."

Everything that Bobby did to showcase his talent was knocked down by someone who felt it to be their duty and obligation to tell him what kind of music he should play. But Bobby knew one thing and one thing only—he owed it to himself to try, to live his dream. It didn't take Bobby long to gather his things and turn the page to a new chapter in his life.

# Chapter Three

## Memphis—A New Beginning

Upon graduation, Bobby knew that it was time to take the next big step in his life. He left home, headed to Memphis and moved in with his brother Billy who had already been there for several years. Within three weeks after his arrival, Bobby got a job at Standard Parts, pulling parts from shelves for the shipping portion of the business. He was working eight hours a day and making $48 a week. This was a long way from that budget sheet in his government class, but he knew he had to make some money so he could record his music.

Bobby felt like he was rocking by the time he left home. But after all of the time that had passed and the conversations that had taken place, Bobby's parents still did not like rock and roll music. In fact, they would not even acknowledge what Bobby was doing—they did not want to hear anything about it. Any time that Bobby brought up his career, they would immediately tell him that he needed to start playing gospel music. They would ignore his enthusiasm for his career, telling him that he did not need to be doing that rock and roll stuff.

Bobby and Billy lived in a two-bedroom house across the street from an uncle and aunt—Huey and Ruth Wood. Billy liked music but did not have the same passion that Bobby had. However, they formed a band called the Starlighters, and Billy was the leader of the band. Their longtime friend from New Albany, Elbert Adair, was in the band with them as well. Bobby sang and played piano, Elbert played guitar, Billy played bass, and another friend, Gene Keller, played drums. Charlie Chalmers played saxophone and Stacy Davidson, Billy Tubbs, and Fred Stewart sang background on all of their songs.

Elbert had already worked with Bobby. So, the Starlighters started practicing. In addition to Elvis and Jerry Lee songs, they were learning songs like "Blueberry Hill" by Fats Domino and "You're the Reason I'm Living" by Bobby Darrin.

During those early years, nightclubs were the rage. If you wanted to hear a really good band you would want to go to one of the better nightclubs in town. For about a year, Billy and his band played the nightclubs in Memphis as well as Mississippi and Arkansas. Their name and style of music had become very well known. A lot of different club owners wanted to hire this talented group of musicians.

After a couple of years playing in different nightclubs, the group landed the Starlight Club, which seated five to six hundred people. The band played there every Friday and Saturday night from 9:00 pm until 1:00 am with a fifteen minute break every hour. The new band name was "The Starlighters featuring Bobby Wood." They played the Top-40 records that were out at the time. The college kids loved it—there were dance contests as well as a full dance floor during the entire show.

Stan Kesler was a great songwriter and steel guitar player in a western swing band. As a songwriter he had some of his songs published. He had written "I Forgot to Remember," "Playing For

Keeps," and "You're Right, I'm Left, She's Gone."

It was obvious that Stan liked the sound that Bobby and his band had produced. Stan asked Bobby if he and the group would be willing to do some recordings at his studio. The group put down two sides that were instrumental. Sides were individual songs that were recorded. They were also learning the Top 40 and rehearsed at Stan Kesler's studio, which was co-owned by Jack "Cowboy" Clement. The studio, Echo Recording, was established for custom recording.

The band would go into the studio and put some songs down. Bobby sang and played piano on the demos. In the first years of being in the studio, every nerve was on edge when the red light went on. No one seemed to remember that you could roll back the tapes and start over. This was something that all the musicians had to overcome. After a while, it was something that would become second nature.

Bobby was both singer and musician for the group. Stan immediately recognized that Bobby's sound was unique and could be developed into something phenomenal. Stan thought that Bobby's voice would appeal to the teenagers. Bobby Wood had a commercial sound, so Stan started looking for songs that would fit Bobby's style.

Stan took Bobby and the band under his wing. He knew that even with their limited experience there was something very special about their sound. The band recorded an instrumental and it was released on a local label where it was played on a few stations. Eventually, Stan began to foster the talent that he saw in Bobby. He saw his potential as an independent artist. The first song that Bobby recorded for Stan was "The Day After Forever.'" It was released as a single and was a regional hit. Jimmy Clanton also released this same song in Texas as a cover record. But this regional hit for Bobby was just what he needed to boost his morale.

The demand for the group to play in Memphis continued to grow. Soon, Bobby's band became the band of Memphis. It wasn't long before the band landed a long-term engagement contract at the Starlight Club. Since the band was the draw, the nightclub owners wanted to ensure that the Starlighters stayed right where they were.

Stan continued to encourage Bobby. At one point Stan took Bobby over to talk to Sam Phillips. Bobby played a couple of Jerry Lee Lewis songs for Sam, but Bobby was still trying to be a Jerry Lee Lewis clone. When Bobby finished playing for Sam, Sam looked at Bobby and simply said, "Bobby Wood, I don't need another Jerry Lee. I've already got one. You go back and bring me Bobby Wood."

Sam was very business-like. He was honest yet very matter of fact. When Bobby heard these comments he was dead silent. His bubble had been burst. He had no response. He was hurt and felt it was a reflection on his talent. Sam went on to tell Bobby, "Find yourself. I am not going to sign somebody that sounds like somebody else."

But as the years passed Bobby realized that Sam had given him some of the best advice that anyone could have offered. He later heard that when Elvis first began, he was trying to sing like Frank Sinatra. Sam gave Elvis the same advice that he had just given Bobby. He told Elvis to sing like Elvis, not like Frank Sinatra.

Bobby told Stan how he felt about the comments that Sam had given him. Stan told him to keep plugging away because he had a great talent. He told Bobby to find his own style and to take the advice to heart. It was good advice—advice that Bobby took. He had the determination to succeed, and he knew that Sam had pointed him in the right direction.

What Bobby realized is that while we all take a little from different artists, we have to be true to ourselves. He learned to listen to others and let it become his own. With that in mind he began his reinvention to find the *real* Bobby Wood.

Bobby worked on developing his own style of music. He knew that his style was funky country with a little bit of gospel and blues mixed in with it. Stan found some songs and even wrote some for Bobby. After a few months, Stan actually recorded Bobby's first record for the Sun label. And what an experience that was! Sam Phillips was everybody's hero in music during those days. By then he had worked with Elvis, Jerry Lee Lewis, Johnny Cash, Roy Orbison, and Charlie Rich. So, to record at Sun was a major accomplishment. To have your name linked to other music legends was extraordinary.

Stan liked the sound that Bobby produced. They recorded two sides. One song was "Everybody's Searchin'" and the other was a song that Bobby does not even remember. But after the recording, Stan told Bobby, "You're getting there with this. That's the Bobby Wood I wanted to hear." They pressed about 200 records. But the real test was the radio and the listening public.

In the 1950's and 1960's the best way to get an idea of what the public would buy would be radio play. Sam took a copy to Dewey Phillips, who was a mega DJ known all over the country. He also took one to George Klein who was a major DJ in the Memphis radio market. If the stations did not get the reaction they wanted, if the phone lines did not light up, then they would not play it. Again, there would be no money spent on the promotion of the song.

The reaction was minimal at best for these first two cuts for Bobby. In fact, these first two sides were never promoted. When Sam Phillips sold Sun Records many years later, the old records that were never promoted were thrown away. No one knew that decades later this recording would be a collector's item of great value. The records that were pressed ended up in the trash. The only two copies that were salvaged ended up with the producer and the writer. And years later, these two guys sold their copies to collectors. As luck would have it, these copies have been dubbed as collector's items under Sun Collections. Since Bobby was listed as a Sun artist, many collectors are now looking for these initial recordings. There have been numerous calls from European collectors. But no one seems to be able to locate any more than the two copies.

Bobby maintained his connection with Stan Kesler and Sam Phillips. He had the opportunity to work with Sam on some sessions before Sam retired from Sun Records. Bobby was asked to work with artists like Harold Dohrman, Ray Anthony and other Sun Label recording artists. There were those "wannabe" singers. Sam would do a session on them but they wouldn't be good enough to be signed. Some of the work was custom work sessions that hired the studio as well as hiring Sam.

Johnny Cash had been on the Sun scene and was making a splash in the music industry. He too was an artist who would etch his name into the archives of music history. But Johnny left Sun Records and signed with Columbia Records in Nashville. Years later in Nashville, Bobby ended up working with Johnny Cash on a lot of his record releases. Even after Johnny left the Sun label, Sam Phillips was still releasing albums of him.

One day, Bobby was asked to come into the studio and do some piano overdubs on some of the Johnny Cash songs that Sam had not released. When Bobby came in, the recording of Johnny Cash and the two guys that played with him didn't tune their instruments to the piano. Sam and Stan came up with the idea of speeding the recording tape up enough to be in tune with the piano. And believe it or not, it worked!

Sam was a marketing genius. He would take a couple of new sides that were on the shelf that had not yet been released and add them to some that had previously been released and bingo—a new album was born.

Bobby began to idolize Sam Phillips and his musical intellect. Working under Sam and watching him do his thing was like going to school or being in a classroom. Sam would direct a new artist to sing from the depths of his soul, and would take him to heights he could only dream of reaching.

His school of thought was simple. A lot of people just didn't get it back then. They didn't realize that music had to touch the soul. Sam once said, "If you don't touch one of the five senses—make people cry, laugh, or dance—then you really haven't done nothin' at all."

Bobby realized that he had learned soul from a soulful master.

Around 1961, while Bobby was working with Stan Kesler and Sam Phillips, a drummer by the name of Gene Chrisman was working with the artist that Bobby had always idolized—Jerry Lee Lewis. But working with Jerry Lee during those days meant a lot of time on the road. Gene was married, and he and his wife, Mary, just had their first child.

Bobby and his band were still playing the Starlight Club at night. The drummer of the group had notified Bobby's brother that he wanted to leave the band and go to dental school. And, as if destiny was already in play, Gene Chrisman was playing for Jerry Lee Lewis that same night after the Starlighters performed. Gene was there to play for that portion of the show. But he also had another item on the agenda. He wanted to hear Bobby and his group, but with one thought in mind. After hearing the band, Gene wanted to become a member.

As soon as the show was over, Gene approached Bobby and asked, "What are the chances of me working with you guys?"

Bobby told Gene that their drummer had just turned in his two-week's notice. That was all that Gene Chrisman needed to hear. Gene told Jerry Lee that he would not be working for him any longer and became a member of the Starlighters. Gene once stated that the Starlighters was the best band he had ever heard in that time period.

Gene and Bobby became more than band members who played together; they became close friends. Bobby had still not set down any permanent roots for living. Gene and his family were living with his grandparents, and Gene asked Bobby if he would like to stay with them for a while. So, Bobby, Gene, and his family, and Gene's grandparents lived in their house on Norris Road for almost two years. Bobby and Gene were content with the arrangement. Bobby had found some people that supported his endeavors in the music field and felt that he had found a home—albeit temporary.

It was during these years that Gene and Bobby began to play sessions at Echo Recording in mid-town Memphis. Stan used Bobby and Gene for the tailored soundtracks. When they weren't working for Echo Recording, they would work at Sun Records with different artists.

# *Chapter Four*

### Gallipolis, Ohio—New Relationships

Woodrow and Margie Saunders lived in the small town of Gallipolis, Ohio. They were the parents of Janice, Joyce, Karen, and Rick. Janice and Joyce were just eleven months apart in age and many thought they were twins. They were so close in both relationship and interests that Woodrow and Margie decided to let Janice begin school the same year that Joyce began just so they could be in the same grade together.

As the girls became older, they both developed an interest and talent in singing. After high school, Janice and Joyce won a talent contest in Columbus, Ohio For the grand prize they went to Cleveland for their own radio and television show for two years. Their stage name became the Tiptoes.

While Janice and Joyce were in Cleveland, they met a girl by the name of Joanne LaBrier. Her aunt owned Crown Electric. Their most notable employee was Elvis Presley. Joanne was dating Ronnie Capone, a distant relative of Al Capone. Ronnie was a drummer for Pepper Recording.

Joanne was impressed with the talent of the two Saunders' sisters. After one of their shows, she sat them down and asked if they would like to go to Memphis. She said that she would introduce them to Red Williams, who was, at that time, a DJ at WREC radio station at the Peabody Hotel.

After much family discussion, Woodrow and Margie decided to take their daughters to Memphis. They knew that these girls loved to sing, and they loved to do it together. They also knew that they had a much better chance of recording in Memphis than in Cleveland.

Cleveland had become more of a pop music town. The most popular songs were by artists like Frank Sinatra and Edie Gorme. Janice and Joyce leaned more toward the style of the Everly Brothers.

So, Woodrow, Margie, Janice, and Joyce packed the car and headed for Memphis. Janice and Joyce were looking for their chance at stardom. They were seeking their dream of a career in music.

Upon arrival, Margie, along with her daughters, met Red Williams. Red was recording at Echo Recording Studio at the time. Red introduced the girls to Stan Kesler. Stan heard these two sisters sing and decided to record them at Sun Studio. One side was "Suspicions" and the other side was "Sisters." After the recording, Stan told Janice and Joyce that he could not spend the time promoting them. Stan's plate was already full.

Janice never thought that she would be the one to sing. In fact, she went to Memphis as more of a favor to her sister. Joyce had a greater dream to sing than Janice did. But destiny kept Janice in Memphis, for she would meet her future husband there.

Joyce made a decision to return to Ohio and eventually took a job working for the State. Janice remained in Memphis and started doing some singing around town—mostly jingles. While she was at Echo Recording, some of the producers heard her sing and began referring her to others.

Janice began to sing background for various artists. One fall day, Janice was singing background, and the Bobby Wood Band was playing on the session. Bobby saw Janice but did not talk to her. To hear Bobby tell the story, he thought she was really stuck up. To hear Janice tell the story, Bobby was not her type at all.

Janice had heard stories about the musicians. Not sure what to believe, who was married and who was not married, she never let herself get close to anyone. She just sang her part and when the session was over, she went to the YWCA where she was living at the time.

But on one particular evening, Janice was working a session that lasted quite late. The "Y" closed at midnight. Mrs. Smith, the supervisor, charged one dollar if anyone was late and she had to get up to open the door. Janice did not want to take the bus. Bobby heard her dilemma and offered to drive her to the "Y."

## Chapter Five

### A New Song

Things were really moving for Bobby, but there was something looming out there—military service. In 1963, Bobby enlisted in the National Guard M.A.S.H. unit in Memphis. His music was on hold during his basic training in Fort Knox, Kentucky. He then came back to his guard unit in Memphis until his military service time was complete, which was one weekend a month for two years.

While in Kentucky, Bobby had a record called "The Day After Forever." It was a Stan Kesler song released by Challenge Records, which was Gene Autry's label. Stan continued to admire Bobby's talent and never looked at him as anything but very special and unique. Military service was not a hindrance to his success.

Time away from the public was and continues to be a scary thing for any artist. Being out of the limelight for any length of time brings a definite amount of uncertainty. You never know if the public will remember you and if they do, will they have the same fondness that they had before?

Bobby loved his music. In 1963, Bobby took a weekend furlough, came home and recorded "If I'm A Fool For Loving You." Stan Kesler wrote the song and knew that Bobby had to record it. "If I'm A Fool For Loving You" was cut at Sun Studio. Bobby was on the piano, Gene Chrisman was on the drums, and a few more musicians were brought in to play on the session. A bass guitar player by the name of Mike Leech was hired and Reggie Young was hired to play guitar. Janice Saunders was hired as one of the background singers.

These guys had a magical sound. Bobby, Gene, Mike, and Reggie blended in a way that was unique in the music industry. They had that soul that Sam Phillips talked about. It wasn't something they had been taught, but it came from deep within each of them. No one knew at that time that the song, 'If I'm A Fool For Loving You,' would be the start of a 50-plus-year career together.

Everyone that heard the song knew it was something special. They knew it was destined to be a big hit. The biggest publishing company in the world at that time was Joy Music out of New York City. They had started a label, Joy Records, with only two artists. One was James Gilreath who had recorded "Little Band of Gold," and the other was Bobby Wood. What had not been anticipated was that "If I'm A Fool For Loving You" would hit the airwaves and become a hit as fast as it did.

The label did not have much distribution set up by the time the song was released. Yet without major distribution in place, the song still reached number one in Birmingham. By the time it had reached number one in Birmingham and was going off the charts, it had caught on fire in Atlanta. This continued from town to town.

"If I'm A Fool For Loving You" stayed in the Hot 100 national record charts for over six months. It would move up and down the national charts like a yo-yo. In every city where it was played, it reached and stayed in the number one slot for as long as eight weeks. Bobby was doing a lot of free promos for this number one hit. Even with the lack of distribution, "If I'm A Fool For Loving You" reached the Top 20 on the national charts.

Bobby Wood was a music phenomenon. People were clamoring to hear this new song, this new talent. Bobby's sound was unique. The teenagers loved it. The adults loved it. Bobby was able to deliver a sound that all America embraced. For every city that played the songs, the radio switchboard would light up for more Bobby Wood.

In 1964, Bobby was out of basic training and started doing a lot of road jobs. He had his own band and they were traveling the mid-south. Bobby's popularity was soaring. It was decided that he needed an agent. Ray Brown was the only real game in town. Bobby signed a contract, and, in 1964, Ray Brown became Bobby's booking agent. Bobby was impressed with Ray's resume. Ray was booking a lot of nightclubs. The pickings had become pretty slim.

Ray was also booking names like Gene Simmons, Ace Cannon, Murray Kellum, Travis Womack, Charlie Rich and many others. These were people who were embraced by the buying public—the people who bought the records.

One day a call came to Bobby from Ray. He wanted to know if Bobby wanted to go on a tour that would pay "pretty good." It was obvious that Bobby needed to go on the road. Ray wanted Bobby to be a part of this tour as an artist; he had booked a series of road jobs for almost a month. But road travel was quite different in the 60's. Ray had hired a band from Detroit. Ray Brown offered his station wagon and Murray Kellum took his car for travel. They would load up Ray's station wagon and hook up with the band members.

These were mainly non-income productive years, but they were necessary. With the contract with Ray Brown, Bobby made 85% and Ray made 15%. But being on the road meant a lot of one-night shows. Traveling with four musicians in one car hauling the instruments in the back was not the rock and roll life style that Bobby had imagined. They stayed in low budget motels. Their travel could be anywhere from three hundred to five hundred miles in one day from one city to the next.

There were some great songs out during this period of time, so the traveling show was quite large. Jay Frank Wilson had released "Last Kiss." He was excited to be on the tour, since he had just had his first number one record. Gene Simmons had released "Haunted House" and it spent some time on the charts as number one. Travis Womack had a big record called "Scratchy" and Murray Kellum had released 'Long Tall Texan.'

Ray Brown knew he had a first-class show. He had the hottest acts of the day and he built a solid tour. Tickets to see these artists were a hot item. They were performing to sold-out audiences in every city.

# Chapter Six

A Life-Changing Moment

Bobby and the group had worked four shows on the Ray Brown tour. The fifth show was in Wheeling, West Virginia. When that show was over, the group decided to leave that night and drive to the next show, which was in Lima, Ohio. Lima was four hundred miles from Wheeling. The guys thought they could arrive in the wee hours of the morning, check into a local motel, and get some sleep before the next show.

Bobby had driven the station wagon for most of the trip. Fatigue and sleepiness had set in, and Bobby realized he was just too tired to drive any further. He pulled over and said, "Somebody else has got to drive." Jay Frank Wilson's manager, Sonley Roush, was riding along with the group. No one seemed particularly anxious to drive during those early hours of the morning. Most of the group had been sleeping.

Sonley finally volunteered to drive. While he drove, Jay Frank Wilson and Bobby were in the front seat with him. Jay Frank was in the middle, and Bobby was in the right front seat. Three of the band members were sitting in the back seat. The instruments and amps were in the back of the station wagon.

Lima was close. The weather had turned cold, and it was very cold inside the car—so cold that the guys asked the driver to turn up the heat. After all, the trip was almost over and everybody was trying to warm up before they had to get out into the cold weather. Jay Frank and Bobby had a pillow they shared between their heads. They were still sleeping off and on knowing that Lima was close.

Roush was still driving, but the fatigue had set in on his body. He had been weaving on and off the road for some time. The car behind Bobby and his group carried Gene Simmons, Murray Kellum, and Travis Womack. They had actually been blowing their horn at Sonley for approximately fifteen to twenty miles down the road. They had seen the car weaving back and forth as it traveled down the highway. In an eyewitness account, they said that Roush had actually gone off of the road on the left hand side. This obviously woke him up because he immediately swerved to get back onto the road.

But that swerve was too sudden, and the driver was traveling too fast. A semi-truck was in the oncoming traffic from the opposite direction. The truck driver had seen what was happening, but there was no way he could react quickly enough. He had basically stopped but there was no place for him to move without causing greater harm. Just before dawn on October 23, 1964, the band members hit the semi-truck head on at a speed of approximately fifty miles per hour.

The instruments that were in the back of the station wagon came flying into the back seat where three band members were sleeping. They immediately awoke and sustained immediate injury. However, they were not hurt as badly as Bobby Wood, J. Frank Wilson, and Sonley Roush.

Seat belts were not installed in cars during those days.

Bobby Wood went through the front windshield of the car. His shoulders kept him from going all the way through the glass but held him in the glass of the windshield. Bobby's face caught the brunt of the injuries. His face was stuck in the glass. One of the band members literally had to pull the door off the car because the door was jammed. They then proceeded to pull Bobby out of the windshield. The entire right side of his face was virtually destroyed. He lost his right eye. Sonley Roush died within a few short minutes after the accident occurred.

Bobby was rushed to a hospital in Lima, Ohio. The paramedics said that Bobby was answering questions as well as giving phone numbers. Bobby had no recollection of that—he went from sleep to shock in an instant.

Upon arrival at the hospital, it was determined that Bobby had lost all but one pint of his blood. He was immediately taken into surgery. During the surgery Bobby went into cardiac arrest. The doctors knew they had lost Bobby. He was rolled into the hallway and covered with a sheet. While on the stretcher, another doctor walked by. At that very moment, one of Bobby's arms came out from under the sheet, falling to the side of the stretcher. Normally, the doctor would pick up the arm and put it back under the sheet.

But in this particular case, something told the doctor to feel for a pulse. When he did, there was a pulse—a faint one—but it was definitely there. Bobby was immediately rolled back into the operating room where his surgery was completed.

After surgery, he remained in a comatose state for the next three days. When Bobby awoke in the hospital he did not know what had happened.

The doctors at the hospital knew who the group was. The accident had hit the UPI wires. Prayers were immediately offered up from everywhere across the United States. People were praying not only for those injured but also for the doctors and nurses who were treating their famous patients. Later Bobby's doctor said that a sudden stillness overcame the operating room. Surgical hands had never done such perfect work; even the assisting physicians were in awe.

Back in Memphis, Paul Bomarito called Janice to tell her that Bobby had been in a tragic accident. Knowing the seriousness of the injuries, Paul actually bought a ticket from another passenger to get Janice on the plane to Lima.

Arrangements were made for Janice to be flown to be at Bobby's bedside. Bobby's brother, Billy, and his dad, Leslie, drove from Mississippi to Lima to be with Bobby. When Janice arrived, Bobby was being wheeled on a gurney from the operating room to intensive care. He had just endured nine hours of surgery and was not recognizable.

Janice came to Bobby's side and looked at him strangely for she was uncertain that this was her fiancé. Then she looked and saw his hands. She knew their size, their shape, and the shape of his nails, she knew for certain that this was Bobby. With the bandages, scars, and disfigurations, his look was so frightening that Janice immediately fainted.

As he came out of his comatose state, the doctors and nurses began asking him if he remembered what happened and why he was in the hospital. Bobby replied, "I don't know, but I think that I have been in a wreck."

The doctor began to explain what happened. He told Bobby that he had been in an accident. He then began to explain the extent of the injuries. Bobby had lost his right eye and would need a prosthetic eye. He had lacerations on the right side of his face as well as a broken jaw.

Bobby was still very medicated. He heard what the doctor said but the information did not register fully. The doctor then asked how well Bobby knew Sonley Roush. He was concerned that this was a close friend of Bobby's and did not want emotional trauma to set in along with the physical injuries. Bobby told the doctor that they had just met for this tour. The doctor then gave him a deep blow—Sonley Roush had died at the accident.

Bobby remained in intensive care for five days. At one point, he raised his left leg to rest his foot on the bed. He immediately felt excruciating pain. After x-rays, doctors discovered that Bobby had a broken leg.

When Bobby was moved from intensive care to a hospital room, he was purposely put in a room with a patient who was paralyzed from the waist down. This patient had no hope, yet he pushed himself every day. The doctors wanted Bobby to see someone who was actually in a condition worse than his own; they wanted him to have hope—the desire to push himself to recovery and eventual healing.

Bobby knew that God was watching over him. As he began to piece information together, one unusual thought came to his mind. Just two weeks prior to the accident, John Franklin, an insurance salesman, sold Bobby a health insurance policy. John heard about the accident and placed a call to the hospital. He assured them that Bobby had full medical coverage. This was a spiritual reminder to Bobby that God takes care of the details in your life when you depend totally on Him.

Recuperation was a long process. After two weeks in the hospital, Bobby was ready to be released from the hospital and return to Memphis. The insurance company leased a private plane and flew Bobby, Janice, and Leslie back to Memphis. The plane flew to a private hanger area at the Memphis airport.

George Klein, a popular Memphis disc jockey, had announced on the radio that Bobby Wood was coming home. When the flight landed and the group deplaned, the sight was overwhelming. Hundreds of people were there. George Klein, whom Bobby had met many years earlier, had always been a good friend and came to give his support. There were friends, family members, and people who knew Bobby from his music—the fans.

There was a car waiting where Bobby, Janice, and Leslie were whisked away to Stan Kesler's home. Bobby remained there for the next two weeks.

Recuperation was long and procedures were tedious. There were numerous plastic surgeries, getting a prosthetic eye made, and dental appointments. The doctors' appointments were constant.

Bobby and Stan would talk about a music return, but Stan kept Bobby focused on healing for his body. At one point Stan told Bobby, "Take one day at a time. Get well first."

Bobby knew that this was what he had to do, but his frustration level rose. In addition, he was still making his National Guard meetings, but he was limited as to what he could do there.

Music never left Bobby's soul, and he never lost the desire to play again. He knew that he had to recuperate, but his passion for music played in his mind every single day. Bobby's full recuperation took almost two years, but he began working nightclubs again within six months. One of his greatest concerns was whether or not he would have the ability to record at the same level as before—and would he have the same level of confidence. Once in the studio, both Bobby and Stan were surprised that Bobby still sounded just like he used to sound—it was as though he hadn't missed a day. The sound was there, and the confidence level was back.

Bobby often tells young artists, "Once you have your first successful venture, your confidence rises to a higher level." With that in mind, Bobby was determined to rise above his circumstances.

There were some regional hits, but nothing big was happening with Bobby's music. It was really difficult to book clubs, caravan, and schedule events without a valid hit on the charts. Most nightclub owners wanted people who had current up-tempo records out. It became increasingly difficult to make a living in the music industry.

Bobby was determined not to let this become a negative life defining moment. While it altered his life for a period of time, he knew that his life had been spared. He knew that he still had dreams to fulfill.

## *Chapter Seven*

A Trip Back Home

Things were going well for Bobby.
"If I'm A Fool For Loving You" had been a mega-hit, topping the charts ahead of Elvis and the Beatles. He had worked with legends. He had several hits out at the time. So it just seemed natural that Ingomar High School would want him to come back to his roots and do a school concert. Of course Bobby said yes.

Bobby took his band to Mississippi. He asked his brother, Billy, to play bass with him. They arrived late in the afternoon, just a couple of hours before the concert. They were both driving their 1960 Cadillacs—Billy in his white one and Bobby in his blue one. They backed those big long cars up to the back door of the gymnasium and began to unload their music equipment.

The stage was set and the equipment was in place. Bobby went to the dressing room to change into his show clothes. Suddenly Bobby looked up, and there, standing in front of him, was his coach—the coach who told Bobby many years ago that he would never amount to anything.

The coach looked at Bobby and said, "What are you doing here, Wood?"

Bobby replied, "I am putting on makeup to cover the scars on my face."

At that point Bobby got up and shook hands with the coach. The coach looked at Bobby and said, "Well, Wood, I guess you made it after all. Right?"

Bobby looked at the coach and responded, "Yeah, I did."

Bobby was proud of how far he had come. He was proud to be at his alma mater playing the concert. He was proud to be standing before his coach proving that he could live out his dreams. At that point in time, Bobby was barely making enough money to put gas in that 1960 Cadillac. But the coach had hurt and humiliated Bobby so badly while he was a student in his class that Bobby was not about to tell him that times were tight. To Bobby, he had made it. He was living his dream. He wanted his coach to know that anything was possible. Bobby held no grudge. The coach saw that same determination on Bobby's face the night of the concert that he had seen in his classroom that day many years before.

The feeling that Bobby had when they took the stage was one of anxiety. Playing to your hometown family and friends is nerve-racking. Somehow the expectations seem greater, almost to a point of feeling a need to be perfect. And perfection in any individual is impossible. Bobby felt that there were so many expectations that night that he could not be himself.

Once the show began, Bobby began to do what he knew how to do—play to a crowd. The first song was finished, and the butterflies began to subside. The reception from the audience was a good one, and Bobby began to be more comfortable and play to his level of performance.

After the show, friends and family members alike were amazed. Bobby Wood, their neighbor, friend, and classmate, had done what he set out to do. There were handshakes and comments of appreciation for the show and for the talent they had seen. Bobby felt gratitude and relief. But there was a great sense of accomplishment that he was able to share at home what he had shared with the world.

## Chapter Eight

### Studio Time in Memphis

Finally, Bobby began doing some studio work again. Most studios in Memphis had their own staff musicians. Other recording companies on the scene were Hi Records and Stax, who had their own staff. And there was Sun Studio. Bobby and Gene Chrisman had again connected with Sun Studio. Mike, Leech and Tommy Cogbill were rotating between Sun and Hi as well as other studios.

In between there might be some recording opportunities at smaller studios, but primarily Sun and Hi were the major recording prospects for these guys. At Sun, Bobby, Gene, Mike and Tommy were recording with artists including Jerry Jeff Walker (Mr. Bojangles), Harold Dohrman, and Billy Lee Riley. Bobby (Emmons) and Reggie were on staff at Hi working with artists that included Gene Simmons, James Carr, Al Greene, and Willie Mitchell.

Occasionally, at Sun Studio, Bobby (Wood), Gene, Reggie, Mike, Tommy Cogbill, and Bobby (Emmons) were put together on sessions. Artists would come into town from Nashville or New York, and they would ask for the "six musicians" together to work with them on their recordings. They knew that with these talented musicians they would have the sound that would get them to the top. Ike and Tina Turner and Solomon Burke were included in some of their earliest lists of recording artists.

In the days of the 1960's many musicians did whatever they could for work. The music scene was flooded with aspiring artists, so they weren't always as picky about taking lower paying jobs. Sometimes they might work and only get $10 per song. It was during that time that the guys met a man by the name of Red West, who happened to be a friend of Elvis Presley. Red had these guys do demo work for him, which proved to be a profitable venture.

Lincoln Wayne Moman, Chips to his friends, was a record producer, songwriter, as well as guitarist. The story is told that Chips nickname comes from his love for gambling. Chips recorded artists including The Marquees and Carla Thomas. He produced the first hit single for Carla Thomas in 1960, a song called "Gee Whiz." He also co-wrote with Dan Penn a song that was recorded by Aretha Franklin called "Do Right Woman, Do Right Man." Another notable song he co-wrote with Dan Penn was "The Dark End of the Street," which was recorded by James Carr.

Musicians and recording studios were popping up all over Memphis. When Chips opened a recording studio in Memphis, he and Bobby made an instant connection. Bobby recorded one of Chips' songs for his new album called *This Time*. Chips played the guitar along side Bobby and new they had a magical sound. Chips often enjoyed playing with Bobby at the different clubs around town.

Bobby and Chips became friends. They had a connection besides that of music. Chips had a Honda motorcycle—one of the first to be released. Bobby had a Sears and Roebuck motorcycle. Bobby and Chips would often be seen riding the streets of Memphis together.

Chips was another person who would prove to be a difference maker for Bobby Wood. His respect for Bobby's talent was obvious. He knew that there was something special about him.

Once Chips had his studio established in Memphis, he called Bobby and asked him if he would take on some of his music projects. One of his major projects at that time was "Big Party" by Barbara and the Browns. Other projects included Goldwax artists like James Carr and the Ovations. He also recorded "Keep on Dancin" by the Gentrys.

As time went on Chips would use more and more of the six guys. He might use one, two, or even three. With these guys together he heard that soulful sound that Sam Phillips talked about and Bobby Wood had become accustomed to in his playing.

During this time Stan Kesler had started a band at Phillips Studio. The band consisted of Charlie Freeman, Gene Chrisman, Sandra Rhodes, Tommy McClure, and Bobby Wood. They were the staff band. Stan would have his group work on special projects that would come up in the studio.

There was another artist who was coming on the scene about this same time—Sam the Sham. Sam had recorded "Wooly Bully" and had used his own band for that session. Then he did a song called "Little Red Riding Hood." Stan knew that the song needed something just a little more to put it over the top, so he called in Bobby and asked him to play piano on it. The song went on to be a smash hit and signature song for Sam the Sham.

Sam and Bobby became close friends. Bobby was still in his recuperation period. He had that noticeable patch on his right eye. Sam wore a trademark turban with a big red ruby right in the front center. He owned an old hearse, which is what he used for his mode of travel.

Sam and Bobby were both working at Phillips Studio one day when Sam asked Bobby if he would like to ride downtown. Of course Sam had on his traditional turban, bearded face, and ring in his ear and Bobby Wood had his eye patch. They proceeded downtown in the antique hearse. Sam parked on a side street of downtown Memphis. Needless to say, they drew a lot of attention from curious onlookers. People either thought they were actually from a gypsy carnival or maybe just freaks. But that didn't stop Sam and Bobby from enjoying the moment.

Chips was still on the scene. He came up with an idea to get Atlantic Records, Bell Records, and Scepter Records, as well as a few others to come to his American studio.

They would bring their artists and use a band that he was going to put together. Chips had asked Bobby to be a part of that band.

Bobby was still tied to Stan Kesler, and he felt a strong loyalty to Stan since he was still his producer. Jim Vieneau was a Nashville producer and the head of MGM Records. Stan and Jim were producing Sam the Sham at the time. Bobby had recently been signed as an artist to MGM. He had recorded a song called "Break My Mind," which was doing well. George Klein had heard the song and loved it. He gave it a lot of radio play in Memphis.

Bobby did not feel that the time was right for him to make that kind of move. But the other guys saw a different opportunity. Gene Chrisman, Reggie Young, Bobby Emmons, Mike Leech, and Tommy Cogbill made the change. They joined Chips in this new venture. Tommy had been working at Phillips as well as Hi during this time. He was known as a great guitarist and became a fantastic electric bass player. Tommy would rotate with Mike on bass guitar. Tommy was one of the best in his field. He played bass guitar on Elvis's 1969 sessions. He eventually went on to produce Merrilee Rush's "Angel of the Morning" and Neil Diamond's

"Sweet Caroline" and "Brother Love." Mike Leech was still in the picture and wrote most of the horn and string arrangements at American Studio for most of the sessions.

Chips knew that he had lured some of the most talented guys in the music business to this new opportunity. But one key element was missing—he needed and wanted Bobby Wood. And so, Chips did not give up on Bobby. He continued his effort to get Bobby to join him and the others.

He told Bobby, "You will make more money than you've ever made in your life."

Bobby's decision was simple. He could either continue with the record artist deal that he had with MGM or move over to American Studio and make enough money to pay the bills. In the long run, the decision wasn't too hard. It was just a question of whether or not to leave Stan. But there were other factors. Bobby's recuperation had been difficult and had him laid up for long periods of time. Then Bobby would be well enough to do a few shows and bring in a little more money, but there were many times that Janice would be the only working member of the family.

It actually took Bobby several months to make this decision. But after mulling over this, Bobby went to Stan and said, "Hey, I've got to make this move, man! I've got to make this move." Bobby did not like the idea of breaking up the staff band at Phillips, but it came down to a matter of survival.

When Bobby arrived on the scene at American, they had already cut "Shake Your Tail Feather," the Purify Brothers, and Arthur Connelly. Bobby came in right after they had cut Dusty Springfield's "Son Of A Preacher Man" for Atlantic Records. Bobby was able to finish out the rest of the sides on Dusty's project.

This was Bobby's first entrance as staff piano player at American Studio. Tom Dowd, Arif Mardin, Jerry Wexler, and

Ahmed Ertigen were all there from Atlantic Records. They just wanted nothing more than the four or five musicians to put down a basic rhythm track and work from there. And this is one thing that stayed with Bobby throughout his career. If the initial tracks feel good then you can always go back and add what you want. A great feeling rhythm track inspires you to hear other things to add, whether it is strings, horns, background vocals, and sometimes nothing. Sometimes it just works out that all you need to do is just release the record.

Bobby has early memories of working with Dusty Springfield. She was not an easy person to get to know. In fact, she seemed very bashful. Bobby did not know what her problems were at the beginning of their working relationship.

One particular day, Dusty was doing her voice warm-ups in an outer office. The band could hear her singing musical scales that were in different keys from the studio. At one point, the band got tickled at her exercises. Members of the band remember her partially singing on some of the tracks. It seemed as though she didn't know the songs. Jerry Wexler told Bobby that she didn't "sing a lick" in Memphis. But most of the band has a different recollection. They remember that she didn't sing final vocals at American but when Jerry and the Atlantic folks went back to New York, Dusty sang the final vocals.

It was only recently that Bobby found out what the real issue was with Dusty. Jerry Wexler wrote about Dusty in his memoirs. He said that she was freaked out about singing on the same microphone that had just been used by Wilson Pickett. Dusty also had some problems about different things and would just withdraw. Wexler also stated that Dusty really did not like being in Memphis. She just couldn't get into the songs. But it was some time later that she came in to Atlantic and she nailed the vocals.

For Bobby, the album for Dusty was the first that he had worked on where they only did simple tracks with not much overdubbing. The Atlantic people left with the tapes, and the next time they heard the finished product was several months later. Atlantic sent the album to the studio. It was put on the turntable in the studio and the band was in awe at the finished product. It was beautiful. The overall, general comment was "Wow!"

# Chapter Nine

### The Hit Factory

This is where history is marked with time.

These six guys just became a hit factory. They were working day and night, and their names were synonymous with hits and success. Most of the time the sessions were quite late. Often times Bobby would not get home until the wee hours of the morning or even daylight. If Chips called at ten o'clock at night, the band had to be ready to get to the studio as quickly as possible for a session. Whether it was a new session or overdubs, they were the group to call, and they were the group at a moment's notice.

The group became so good and worked in sync so well that demand for their talent and expertise became greater and greater. They would be there for sessions, but Chips also wanted them to be present for string and background overdubs.

When Bobby first came over to American they were playing rhythm and blues songs. Gene Chrisman and Bobby Wood were used to playing rock and roll, which is on the top of the beat with your hair on fire.

Bobby was faced with learning a new way of playing. Musicians called this a laid-back rhythm and blues beat. Bobby wasn't sure he was going to be able to adapt his style, because it was so laid back. But in true Bobby Wood fashion, he not only picked up this style, he mastered it, just like he did with every song and every style of music he ever played. He had just come from gospel, to rock and roll, to R and B and pop.

Because Bobby had been so busy with long hours in the studio, he had completely missed one of the artist's hits. One day an artist had come back in to work on his second album, but Bobby didn't even know his first single had reached number one. His name was BJ Thomas. That first single Bobby had played on was "Hooked On A Feeling."

He didn't have time to listen to the radio or look at the Top-100 charts and by this time he had dropped his dreams of being an artist. Bobby once said, "I am really not a good road puppy. I just didn't like the road that much."

He would record until the early hours of morning, sleep until noon, then reappear for the next session.

American Studio had three producers at one time. In addition to Chips, there was also Dan Penn who had already produced the Boxtops. Tommy Cogbill was producing Neil Diamond and Merrilee Rush. With the three producers there were also three writers. One writer, Mark James, had connected with a couple of huge hits. He wrote "Hooked On a Feeling" that was recorded by BJ Thomas. He also wrote "Suspicious Minds" that would become an Elvis signature song.

During this time Bobby was also singing background for American. Chips would put a group together and Bobby would be there in between his time with sessions. At one time, Paul Davis came into American and Bobby sang background along with a fellow writer and musician, Johnny Christopher. While he was working on these projects he was introduced to Neil

Diamond.

Working with Neil was a real learning process. Bobby was not familiar with Neil or his music. When Neil came into the studio, he had some songs with him that he wanted to record. But the band had one goal in mind—finding a hit, just like they always did.

As Tommy Cogbill, the producer, and the band listened to these songs; they all reached the same conclusion. These songs were not great and did not reach the same level as the other hit songs they had recorded. They recorded "Holly Holy" and "Brother Love's Traveling Salvation Show." Bobby thought these two songs were "pretty good." In reminiscing, Bobby remembers that on "Brother Love," Neil wanted Bobby to play a southern gospel feel on piano. This didn't take much effort on Bobby's part because that was his background. It worked!

Mike Leech and Bobby started a bass line together on "Holly Holy." Once again Bobby played to his calling on the intro. Bobby was dubbed the intro and ending specialist. After the tracks were laid on tape, Tommy didn't seem really impressed with either song. At one point he even asked Neil if he had anything else.

Neil said he had started a song called "Sweet Caroline" but hadn't finished the lyrics. Tommy asked him to play and sing what he had. When Neil sat down and began to play and sing this song, everyone knew from the start that "Sweet Caroline" was something special. The band began to put down a track with the lyrics still unfinished. Neil approached Bobby and asked what Bobby thought of a lick that would be played in the chorus.

Bobby thought it was a good line and he played it on the track. When the track was finished they went into the control room. There sat Tommy Cogbill who was grinning from ear to ear. He looked up and said, "There's your hit!" One person was not convinced—Neil Diamond. In fact, he didn't have much to say. But with some changes, Neil recorded the song and once again the musicians' ears heard a song that would be etched in music history. Of the three songs, "Sweet Caroline" was the hit. "Holly Holy" and "Brother Love" were big records but they didn't go as high on the charts as "Sweet Caroline."

## *Chapter Ten*

Memories from the Sound Room

There were a lot of memories outside of just picking a good record, playing on a session, or even meeting famous artists. Often times, unusual things would happen that were just worth remembering.

On one very late night, the band was upstairs in the studio office. The rhythm section was there to help with string and horn overdubs. While the overdubs were being done in the studio, the band members were upstairs in the office, sitting on the floor playing cards. They had an office above the Ranch House, which was a restaurant next door. To get to the office that was located on the east side of the building you had to go by way of a set of metal stairs. The office had been broken into several times. Most of the studios in Memphis were in a bad part of town, so all of the guys packed guns. Cars were being broken into, people were robbed, and crime was high in this area.

It was pretty cold on this particular night. All of the guys were playing cards, but they all had their coats with them. Suddenly, there was a creak on the stairs, then another creak, and then another. It appeared that someone was sneaking up the stairs, probably getting ready to break into the office. From the sound, or lack of sound at this point, they all knew that someone was standing outside the office door. They also knew that there was no other option for getting away except by way of the stairs. Since it was so quiet, the guys determined that the perpetrator must be right outside the door. So, young, invincible Bobby Wood got up, eased over to his coat and grabbed a thirty-eight revolver out of his coat pocket. With the pistol in his right hand, he caught the door bolt with his left hand. With one swift move, opened the door quickly and found himself with his pistol barrel right on the nose of a policeman.

The policeman started yelling, "Hold it! Hold it! Hold it!" It was never determined who was more frightened, Bobby or the policeman. Bobby quickly put the gun back in his coat pocket.

The anxious and embarrassed policeman looked at Bobby and said, "Hey, buddy, you had better put that gun away before I remember that you had it."

During those days you could have a gun to protect yourself at your place of business, but it scared the heck out of Bobby and the cop. A friend of one of the band members was a police lieutenant. It was one story that he never let Bobby forget. But as the story goes, the policemen at the precinct were laughing for quite a while.

You had to find some humor in what you did as a studio band. Laughter was truly the best medicine to relieve tension and bring lighter moments for what were often some very long days. The band was together a lot and had a good time no matter what they were doing.

One time five of the guys were cutting a session on a group called the Blossoms. They were three black singers who were not from Memphis. They were at the studio, and the building was just not in the best condition. In fact, the building had become rat infested. There were times when the guys would be in the middle of a session and they would have to stop recording. The rats would be mating in the ceiling. The squealing would be so loud that the band would have to stop recording until the rats would settle down.

Finally, an exterminator was called to deal with the rats. Most of them were dead but during a session with the Blossoms—right in the middle of their song—a big, old rat came waddling across the floor. You could tell from his movement that he was old and half dead. The first person to see it was Bobby Emmons, but he just kept on playing. Almost immediately and in sync, the Blossoms all saw the rat at the same time.

There were some bar stools that the bass players sat on that were about waist high. Almost in unison, those three girls were each standing on a bar stool screaming as loud as they could.

Bobby Emmons got up from the organ, picked up a broom from the corner of the room, and whacked the rat on the head. He then picked up the rat by the tail, threw him in the garbage can and then walked back over to the organ and started playing again. It took the Blossoms a while to get off those stools. There were no more rats during their session, but it took those three ladies a while to get their breath. The laughter continued for quite some time.

Nights were often very long. Recording sessions often began in early afternoon and went on until the wee hours of the morning. The band would usually be at the studio at noon, go eat, and then begin to get into the project at hand, whether it was demos for the writers or master sessions. More often than not, fatigue would set in and playing almost became robotic. It was during those times that even humor did not find its place in the session and just didn't seem to work under any circumstances.

There was one particular night in the studio when the session began quite late. Soon the clock ticked on four o'clock in the morning. Bobby had reached a point that he felt like he really could not go on any more.

As he described it, "My spirit came loose from my body and it was like I was standing there watching myself play. I was looking at my hands move but it seemed like I was looking from a distance." He thought, "Man, I have got to get out of here." At that point Bobby went and washed his face. He looked at himself in the mirror and thought, "Man, this is too weird."

He packed up and went home. The session was over.

Some of the other members of the group had those same moments. On one night in particular, one of the guys was so tired that he went out back to the parking lot, leaned against his car and began to cry uncontrollably. Once he started it just seemed as though he was never going to stop.

These guys were in such demand. But with that demand came long hours to a point of being overworked—staying up all night and all day—their mind, playing tricks on them because of being totally exhausted.

## Chapter Eleven

### Learning the Ropes

With all of the exposure on the Top-100 charts, word traveled fast that this band could "make it happen." They had the ear for a hit song and the ability to know what instruments would give a song the sound the public wanted to hear.

When "Sweet Caroline" was in the finishing stages, the melody line was originally the piano melody line. Neil Diamond wanted Bobby to play the piano line, but the decision was later made to take the piano out and put the horns on the line. The piano was pulled down and replaced with horns. Bobby, Paul Davis, and Johnny Christopher sang background. The changes were made and the song was a smash hit. That's the way records were done in those early days. The guys would look at each other and "just fix it."

Sometimes a unique sound might be needed to give a song that "over the top" edge that would make it not just a release but also a hit song. These guys were as creative as they came. They would look for those small things that would make the records unique. In those days, they would find some "instrument" to play or something to beat on—whether it was a bean pot, tape box, or spoons on the floor—they would find a way to make it happen.

Sometimes finding the exact sound that was needed could take hours. When the band was working on "Hooked on a Feeling" by B.J. Thomas the sound that Chips was looking for just wasn't there. There happened to be a bean pot, tape box, and tambourine in the studio. Gene, Mike, and Reggie just started beating on this pot, and these other "instruments" looking for the magical sound. They continued to look around studio and find things that could be improvised to give them what they were looking for. Each one of the guys was on a different microphone and they worked until the perfect sound came through the speakers.

While "Just Can't Help Believing" was being overdubbed, the track had already been laid down on tape. They left the middle portion of the song empty when the track was done. They were trying to determine what instruments should be played or overdubbed for that section of the song. They went into the studio and began working on something to fill in that space. Reggie ended up playing the first part on the guitar and Bobby played the second half on the piano. That was it! Another successful overdub! Another sound that made the song unique and the artist had another hit! They did it again!

During the recording session for Dusty Springfield's "Windmills of Your Mind," Bobby raked his hand across the strings of the inside of the piano. One of the guys held the piano sustain pedal down and Bobby raked his hands across the strings again. Perfect sound! Perfect effect!

The band always played to the artist and to the song, which made all of those records identifiable. From the first note you knew who the recording artist was and what the song was. The band had a saying, "If it doesn't add anything, don't play it." There were many nights that the band would spend hours trying different ideas. Sometimes these ideas worked and sometimes they didn't. What they were looking for was originality, something that would add an exceptional sound.

The computer world today has often taken away the individuality of the artist as well as the soul of the music.

It became more important for that sound to be right. Not only did the band record the music, they now had part of the production at the studio. The production company was American Group Productions. So all of these guys were present for everything including final mixing of the song. Now there was money from recording as well as a small percentage on the sales of the records. That was the beginning of the band sharing production royalties. It was during this time that the band was dubbed the 827 Thomas Street Band, for the address of the studio. It started with a few credits—acknowledging the producers and the 827 Thomas Street Band.

The 1960's were bringing a lot of talent and a lot of hit records. At that time no credits were given to musicians from the record labels. But the 827 Thomas Street Band was one of the first to receive label credits.

While the band was learning the ropes on the business end, their most important lesson came inside the studio. They learned to play together as a band, as one unit. They had respect for each other's talents, and they learned not to be individual stars but to work as a group. They learned that as six guys with six very unique abilities in music, they were powerful and a force to be reckoned with in the music world.

As they had discussed with each other many times, the number in the band was not significant. It was what they each brought to the table. And they all agree that they never stepped over the line or got in each other's way. They had respect for each other from the very beginning. Each member contributed to the talents of the others. They always gave 110% regardless of the project.

## *Chapter Twelve*

### The Comeback of Elvis Presley

There were a lot of artists coming through the studio to record with the 827 Thomas Street Band. At this time, Elvis was not the hottest artist in the world. He was down to approximately 200,000 in record sales. Elvis was primarily doing the songs that were in his publishing company which were in his movies. This was not the Elvis that had hit the scene in the 1950's. The public just wasn't buying it. They wanted the originality and magnetism of the young man from Tupelo who burst onto the music scene with that soulful sound.

Elvis was such a gifted musician and artist. He had heard and liked the songs by the Box Tops. He really liked "Hooked on a Feeling," by B.J. Thomas. Neil Diamond, Wilson Picket and Joe Tex were all capturing the public's ear. And the 827 Thomas Street Band was working with all of them.

Elvis was getting bored with his own material. He took pride in his music and his accomplishments, but he wanted to move forward and give the public what they expected to hear from someone of his caliber. His people had to figure out a way to get into that groove.

There was a meeting with Elvis and his inner circle at Graceland a week before the decision was made to record at American. According to Marty Lacker, Elvis and Felton Jarvis were making plans to go with another Nashville recording session. During this discussion it was suggested that Elvis Record at American and look for better songs. After lengthy discussions, Elvis made the decision to record at American. Elvis and Felton asked Marty if recording could begin the following Monday.

Marty called Chips and asked if he would like to record Elvis the following Monday. Chips response was, "Definitely, yes!" Chips said, "I have Neil Diamond scheduled but I will rebook him."

The deal was done.

Elvis loved the music of the decade. His beginnings were in Memphis, and his early records had the groove, the soul, and the blues. He was missing that part of his musical heritage.

The 827 Thomas Street Band had 19 number ones under their belt and 117 chart records including Herbie Mann's "Memphis Underground," which was jazz. In fact, that album was in the *World Book Encyclopedia* because it was number one as the longest running jazz records that stayed number one for that length of time. It was on the charts for over five years, with much of that time at number one. The 827 Thomas Street Band was riding on a string of success.

Bobby Wood was told that Elvis was coming into the studio. He began to really get a case of nerves. Bobby had his ego in check, and, in order to settle himself down, he reminded himself that the band had more hits on the charts at that time—they were hotter! There was no reason to get nervous about working with Elvis Presley. Wrong!

Elvis had a certain level of magnetism. He had a charisma

that was unmatched in the music industry. Somehow everyone knew when he arrived in the parking lot in the back of the studio. When he and his crew walked in the back door of the studio, the whole place choked. Every single person was rendered speechless.

When Elvis came in, he and his entourage walked toward the control room. He stopped at one point and said, "What a funky, funky studio." He proceeded to walk to the control room where Felton and Chips were sitting. He then came back into the studio and shook hands with every single person. He had a gift for putting everyone at ease. He had charm, and, as the women would attest, he was easy on the eyes. He was a really good-looking guy as well, dressed in a navy blue leather outfit with his Elvis-style white shirt that had a big collar. He made a statement with his clothes. He didn't even have to speak—with just his mere presence in the room you knew that Elvis was "in the building."

The entourage included all of those who moved in his circle, his publishing group, and the RCA representatives. The publishers brought in a stack of acetate dubs and started playing them for Chips and the 827 Thomas Street Band to hear. When Bobby heard the songs, he immediately knew that it was just more of the same. It was the same sound that had brought him down to 200,000 in record sales.

The whole time these songs were being played, Elvis watched for the reaction from the band. Body language speaks volumes. The band was standing there listening with as much respect as they could muster. But, their inner voices were asking, "Do we have to go through this?"

George Klein was a close friend of Bobby's and knew that he had that special ear for music. He walked over and very quietly asked Bobby what he thought of the songs that were being played? Knowing that he had to tell the truth, Bobby said, "I think they're a piece of crap."

George Klein immediately turned to Elvis and repeated what Bobby had said. Bobby was shocked to say the least. He looked at George and said, "Thanks a lot!"

Bobby was uncertain and somewhat apprehensive about the reaction that Elvis would have. Did Elvis want the truth? Did he want to be told the music was great? Bobby watched for a reaction but he didn't get what he expected.

Elvis began to laugh. He looked at Bobby and knew that Bobby was telling the truth. Elvis was no fool and he agreed. The conclusion at that previous meeting was that he had bad material. So, with Bobby's comment as his affirmation, he knew that Bobby was on target with his comment. He also had a renewed sense of purpose to catapult himself back to the top of the music world.

Chips Moman was still in the picture. Chips began to play some things that had come to him. Things he knew would capture Elvis's attention and the public's heart. Everyone knew that "Suspicious Minds" would be a hit. It had the soul, the blues, and the energy that Elvis needed. Because everyone involved knew it was a hit, there was a scuffle with the publishing people over the song. Apparently the publishers were strong-arming Chips to give them at least one-half of the publishing.

Finally, Chips just blew up and said, "Hey, you just go ahead and take Elvis out of here because you are not getting any publishing on this song."

From there things just began to unravel. There were several other sides that had been cut at that point in time, most of which was of lesser importance than "Suspicious Minds." But Elvis really liked what was being recorded.

Then Elvis heard "In the Ghetto" and he knew it was a hit song. Although Colonel Tom Parker did not like the song, Elvis loved it. Mac Davis was brought in to play the song. When people would get in the presence of Elvis Presley, there was an awe struck demeanor that everyone had. Mac Davis was no exception. When he was playing the guitar and singing "In the Ghetto," his hand was actually trembling. That's just the effect that Elvis had on people.

Elvis was sitting behind the control board with Chips and Mac was sitting on the couch in front of the control board playing "In the Ghetto."

About half way through, Elvis turned around and shook his head in affirmation. Elvis knew it. The band knew it. This was a smash hit!

Waiting in the wings was "Kentucky Rain" that had been written and sent by Eddie Rabbit. Bobby Wood stood out on that session. George Klein states, "When Bobby played that left hand—those left-handed keys on "Kentucky Rain," you knew you had something special." Klein further states, "The studio separates the men from the boys. With Bobby Wood and the rest of those guys, you knew you would have a hit. In the studio you can't fake it. There are just so many examples of what a great blend Elvis and the Memphis Boys were together."

As George Klein has often told in his stories about Elvis, "The musicians wanted to see Elvis get a number one record as much as Elvis wanted it for himself. Elvis and this band had a great blendship." Elvis knew that the musicians were not going to play half way and Elvis never did anything half way. They all put their heart and soul into the music."

Then there was "Don't Cry Daddy." Elvis knew that he found the magic again. He had a great ear for music and he knew it when he heard it. Everyone involved was watching for Elvis's reaction to every song. People always watched to see what Elvis was going to do or say. To be in the company of Elvis Presley was a surreal experience. He always was and always will be known as the King of Rock and Roll.

As the story is told, Marty and Elvis were in the car together along with members of his entourage. Elvis leaned forward and punched Marty on the shoulder and said, "I think we've got something great!" Marty said, "I think you're right."

This music clearly put Elvis right where he wanted to be—on top. *Rolling Stone* magazine later affirmed that *Elvis In Memphis* was selected as one of the top 500 albums of all time.

Elvis was a very cordial and warm person. On one particular night Bobby was in the studio. Things were a little quiet and Bobby was fooling around on the piano. Elvis came out and sat down next to Bobby. They sat there—side by side—and talked for 30 minutes or longer. They talked about going to church. They talked about living the Christian life. Elvis always had a strong desire to talk about his faith as well as his love of singing gospel music. Gospel music touched his soul. Elvis knew what the Christian life was supposed to be like.

He shared his stories about Hollywood and how all of the temptations were so great, yet they were against everything that he believed in. Elvis wanted to hear Bible truths. He had a real desire to grow in Christian faith. In fact, those were some of his favorite times. In retrospect, Bobby realized that Elvis embraced those times where the conversations were real—times where he could share his faith and feelings with someone who was genuine.

Looking back, Bobby said, "I realize that my relationship with Elvis was obviously stronger that I knew at the time. Elvis seemed to be comfortable with me, kidding around with me."

Bobby was still wearing his eye patch at the time. Elvis found out, through George Klein, why Bobby wore the patch. At that point in time, Elvis started calling Bobby Mr. Wiley. Will Roger's pilot was Wiley Post. In those late night recording sessions, Bobby recalls how Elvis would look over and say, "Hey, Wiley, is the plane warmed up?" Bobby's response was always, "Yea, it's ready to go."

Even though Elvis joked with Bobby about the patch, George

Klein had related the information about the accident and the seriousness of it. George had told Elvis that Bobby was still going through plastic surgery at that time. Then George told Bobby something that amazed him. Elvis offered his plastic surgeon and was willing to pay for all surgical costs. Bobby told George, "I really appreciate that offer. In fact, it's fantastic! But I'm about finished with my surgery, but the offer was one that I will never forget."

When Elvis would come into the studio, he never liked to get down to work immediately. He shook hands with all of the band members, told them how much he appreciated them playing on his sessions, and would begin to warm up. His choice for those warm-ups was gospel music. It just tied to his faith, his beliefs that he had talked about so many times with Bobby, and his love for the music of his soul.

Elvis was always encouraging others. He told Bobby how much he had enjoyed the records the 827 Thomas Street Band had recorded—from the Boxtops to B.J. Thomas to Dusty Springfield.

One day when Elvis was in town, he discovered that the band was recording with Roy Hamilton. Roy happened to be one of his heroes. Elvis called Chips and asked if he could come to the studio and bring Roy a song that he had. The song was titled "Angelica" and was recorded by Roy that day. This in itself was unusual. The recording session was during the day and it was odd for Elvis to leave the house during daylight hours.

Dan Penn found out that Elvis was coming into the studio. He called Chips and asked if he could come into the studio with his new Polaroid camera. Chips' response was yes. Elvis wanted pictures with the band and with Roy. Elvis counted it as an honor to be photographed with this band, a group he considered to be legends, and he had the highest regard for Bobby. It was later written in an interview that Elvis gave when he stated his opinion of Bobby. He said, "Bobby Wood is the most commercial piano player that I have ever heard." He knew Bobby had something special. They built strong connections—a connection for true talent, a connection of respect.

Elvis didn't usually begin his recording sessions until ten o'clock in the evening at the earliest, and some nights it might be as late as midnight before he arrived. One night the band was waiting for Elvis to come in and record. The call finally came and the message was surprising. Elvis had worked so hard that he lost his voice. There would be no recording with Elvis that night.

Chips had already slated "Don't Cry Daddy" for that night. Chips wanted to go ahead and do a track without Elvis. Chips said, "Bobby can do the pilot vocal." There was just one problem with that scenario—they didn't know the right key for Elvis.

Elvis's voice was an incredible instrument. Bobby asked Chips to play one of the songs they had previously recorded. After the tape was played a couple of times, Bobby figured out where Elvis's voice range was. That range was one step lower than Bobby's range, so Bobby did the pilot vocal with the band, but dropped it a step lower. It wasn't easy for Bobby to perform the song in a key that was a step lower, but he did it well enough for a great track.

When Elvis finally came to put his voice on the track he asked, "How did you guys know what key would be right for me?" Chips related the story to Elvis. He explained how Bobby solved the problem. Elvis said, "Wow, the key is perfect." He was again amazed at the musical ear and sense of sound and pitch that Bobby had.

While the band was in awe of Elvis, Elvis was in awe of the band's work. Elvis always gave every bit of himself in every recording session. He worked as hard if not harder than the band. He was totally into every project, but he later said that working at American Studios and with this band were some of the most enjoyable sessions that he ever remembered doing.

Everyone there was committed, and that commitment paid off even more than anyone could have imagined. The band worked diligently with Elvis and in a two-week time period; they recorded twenty-eight sides that included some of Elvis's most recognizable hits.

Elvis and Bobby continued to build their special relationship. They enjoyed the times that they had to sit and just talk to each other. One late night when they were sitting in the control room, Bobby noticed a ring that Elvis was wearing. It was full of diamonds, rubies, and sapphires. Bobby commented to Elvis that he liked his ring. Elvis pulled it off his finger and handed it to Bobby. Bobby looked at the ring and said again that it was a beautiful ring. As Bobby handed the ring back to him, Elvis said, "It's yours."

Bobby replied, "Elvis, I am not taking your ring. I was just admiring it."

Elvis wanted Bobby to have that ring. Bobby had to literally talk Elvis out of giving his ring away. That is just the kind of person that Elvis was—his focus was not on money or things. His focus was on people. Bobby felt both privileged and honored to call him his friend.

Then one shocking day, a day that no one even thought about, the devastating news came in. Elvis Presley died on August 16, 1977.

Bobby said, "It was like knocking the breath out of me. I was recording an album with Joe Tex. Someone from the control room stopped the session and called us all into the control room." Wood continues, "Buddy Killen told us that they had just gotten the news that Elvis had died. There was complete silence. Some of the men were moved to tears. At that point, the session stopped and everyone left. Very few words were spoken. The next day we got another phone call. Buddy told us that Joe was so shaken up that he just couldn't record that day." He added, "Joe was one of

Elvis's biggest fans. It really hit him hard."

Bobby then added, "So many things went through my mind. I had lost a great friend. I thought of all of the times that we spent together and how special they were. He was just an amazing person and wonderful friend."

Even today, the Memphis Boys have traveled Europe doing the American recordings for the Elvis Fan Clubs. After all of these years, the fans have deemed Elvis's Sun records and the American Studio records as his best. RCA executives stated that these records are the all-around best sessions that Elvis Presley ever cut. Each of these records were created in Memphis by the people that played and felt soul.

Soul matters in music. It always has and always will.

The remarkable part of the continuing story of the Memphis Boys is that fans worldwide still follow this group of extraordinary musicians any time they perform an "Elvis show." In a recent autograph session at Graceland there were fans from every corner of the globe standing in line to see the Memphis Boys. There were generations of family members—people who had grown up with Elvis and had heard the music that was recorded at American Studio. These fans have introduced their children to this music and the talent of the Memphis Boys as well.

And it was that music that defined his comeback. Those fans boldly acknowledged that Elvis and the Memphis Boys made his "best music ever." Fans clamor for tickets and shows by this talented group of musicians. Bobby often hears from Elvis Fan Club presidents and members alike from around the globe. The common question is, "Where will you be next? When is your next Elvis show?" The enthusiasm has never died for Elvis or the band that played with him on those historical records.

## Chapter Thirteen

A REFLECTION ON FAMILY

Bobby Wood had met Janice Saunders in 1962. To make ends meet, Janice took a few jobs in different places around town. In fact, she worked as a seamstress and she didn't know how to sew. She also worked in cosmetics at a local department store and learned how to sell and apply make-up. Whatever it took—Janice was a survivor.

Janice also ended up singing and doing background vocals with a lot of people all over town. One day Hershel Wigginton was getting a group together to sing background for Fats Domino at a local supper club. Fats was one of her heroes. Janice was standing there singing background on Blueberry Hill and had tears running down her face. She was singing for a great music legend. Bobby thought Janice was talented, but he also thought she was a little stuck up. Janice was not impressed with the band members, perhaps judging them on their appearance, as they would walk into the studio with holes in their jeans, duck tales, and just an overall grungy look. Janice thought that this band was good but at the same time—to her—they seemed kind of trashy.

However, studio time was fun. Bobby has always been known for his sense of humor. So, laughter was one of the main things that Bobby and Janice shared together. This shared humor went off and on between the two of them for a while. When Bobby would be in the studio and Janice was there, the evening would end up with them eating somewhere and just spending the night laughing. Then, five or six months would pass before they worked together again. It just seemed that they were two people who, when together, could have a really good time.

Bobby and Janice seemed to be content (occasionally) spending time together—sharing time after working sessions. It was more than that, though. Bobby thought that she was the most beautiful girl that he had ever seen. She had values, morals, and everything that he considered important in a person.

Janice lived at the YWCA in Memphis. The pair would ride around in his 1954 black Cadillac Coupe deVille, and then Bobby would take her home to the "Y." Quality time seemed very important, especially with the whirlwind of studio life always present. At some point Bobby knew that Janice was the person that he wanted to spend the rest of his life with—to be his life partner. They eventually made plans to get married—someday.

After the wreck, Janice flew to Lima, Ohio. She was at Bobby's side day and night. As seconds became minutes, minutes became hours, and hours became days, Janice held her vigil at Bobby's side. In fact, she spent her 24th birthday at his bedside, praying for his recovery. She was not going to leave her fiancé (her best friend) until he could come back to Memphis with her.

The UPI wires were saying that Bobby's condition was very grave. People all over the world were praying for Bobby and survival was questionable for a while, but finally a turn for the better came.

As Bobby rallied in the hospital, the time finally came that he was physically able to return to Memphis. With the pilot, Bobby's dad, and Janice, Bobby came home to a huge welcome at the airport. When Bobby stepped off that plane in Memphis with Janice at his side, the emotions were overwhelming. Throngs of people saw their answer to prayer standing in front of them. Bobby and Janice made their way through the crowd and went to the home of Stan Kesler for a time of recuperation.

Bobby realized one dream, immediately. He had met Janice Saunders several years ago, and she had been by his side during the highs and lows, and had been by his side during those long days in the hospital in Lima, Ohio. The couple had talked for quite a while about marriage and their commitment to each other was solid and firm. This accident had no bearing on their future together.

So, with life and all of its uncertainties, Bobby and Janice did not want to wait any longer to get married. They both knew that they simply wanted to be together. Bobby's accident was on October 23$^{rd}$ and on November 15$^{th}$ of that same year; Bobby Wood and Janice Saunders were married. They asked the minister if he would marry them after the morning service, so they were married on that Sunday afternoon after church.

When the preaching was over, the minister said, "Well, we've got a couple here that comes to this church all of the time. Those that want to stay around, they are fixin' to get married." With the congregation in place, a wedding was held.

Janice made a beautiful bride, but Bobby was not your typical dapper-looking groom. Bobby made it down the aisle with a cast on his left leg, stitches on the right side of his face, and a patch over his right eye.

In typical-wedding fashion, some decided to follow tradition and decorated their car. By this time, Bobby had a 1960 Cadillac Sedan deVille. A few days after the wedding, he took his car to the local service station to get the "Just Married" washed off. When Bobby got out of the car, the station attendant looked at him with surprise, laughed hysterically and said, "Boy, it didn't take her long. What did she use—a frying pan?"

Bobby and Janice often laugh as they remember the expression of the desk clerk when they checked into the local motel for the honeymoon.

The pair tried to make ends meet while living in a very small duplex in east Memphis. A lot of their time was focused on setting up their new household; furniture was the major purchase needed. During this decade, most banks frowned on musicians because they did not consider the music industry a legitimate way to make a living. However, a close friend, C.D. Smith, sent them to the bank where he did his business. On his word alone, the bank gave Bobby and Janice a $1000 loan, and with that loan they purchased four rooms of furniture—a living room, dining room, and two bedrooms all early American style.

Bobby finally got a road job that took him to Texarkana, Arkansas. After he paid the motel bill, gas expenses, and paid the band, he ended up with about $100 in his pocket.

Bobby knew that he had a place in the music world. With Janice by his side, he was determined to find it. In November of 2009 he and Janice celebrated forty-five years of marriage.

They now have two children and five grandchildren, they still laugh together and share the same love for music of the heart and soul.

Chris is the older of their two sons. He is in the Air Force Reserves flying T-38's as a pilot instructor, and he is a civilian pilot for FedEx. He and his wife Angie have two sons, Austin and Tyler, and a daughter, Ashley, and they reside in Tennessee.

Aaron is the second born son. He rode bareback for the PRCA circuit for several years and met his soon to be wife, Kelly, while on the rodeo circuit. Aaron decided that he had to support a family, so he gave up the rodeo life and is now a firefighter and soon-to-be paramedic. He and his wife have one son, Rylan, and one daughter, Taylor, and they currently reside in Colorado.

Bobby has often said, "You are away from family so much in this business. You don't get to see your kids grow up the way that you really want to—that's the down side of this business."

Bobby never liked being away from family as much as he was, but his family was always his most important priority. He wanted to be a good provider but an even better husband and father. He always valued the time with his family and learned to treasure each moment.

*Chapter Fourteen*

A Business Like No Other

The music business is like no other business, yet at the same time, it is the same as many others. Once you meet someone, you never know when he will cross paths with you again—or what kind of impact he will have on you.

Bobby worked with Stan Kesler and Jack Clement when they owned Echo Recording Studio in Memphis. It was during those days that Bobby met Allen Reynolds. When Allen and Bobby first met, Allen was still in college. Even though he had an interest in music, Allen went on to pursue business interests. After all, he had a wife and baby to support, so music became a part-time venture. But Allen kept some of his ties to music and never lost that interest.

Allen had become a bank branch president in Memphis. Bobby would often stop by and talk to him for hours on end. While he continued his banking career, Allen was still rapidly developing his musical abilities. Bobby was a part of the 827 Thomas Street Band and tied to Chips Moman. Allen says, "Bobby was a part of the rhythm section on Thomas Street.

Bobby, Reggie Young, and Gene Chrisman and that group were my heroes. They were making their living in music, and I just thought that was the greatest thing in the world."

He was writing with Dickie Lee and Jack Clement. Allen had a natural musical talent, and, for a while, he, along with Bobby, Janice, and Sandra Rhodes would be hired to sing background for different artists. Allen was also writing songs. He had a hit song called "Five O'Clock World" while he was still working for the bank. He spent a couple of years in the music business but banking was earning him a living and had been for the past five and a half years. But like so many others with a passion for music, Allen's greatest desire was to be back in the music world.

Reynolds says, "I never gave up the music. I was still writing songs, and I would get Bobby to come over and play on the sessions for the songs that I had written. I knew how good Bobby was and wanted him in on my projects."

Allen continues, "Bobby was playing with Chips, and Chips did not want anybody from his band playing for anybody else. But Bobby would come on over and help me out anyway. That's just how Bobby was. I just loved him. It was obvious from the beginning that his musicality—that was just a part of his being."

In the late sixties, Allen Reynolds decided that Memphis was not going to be the place for him if he was going to make it in the music industry. Times were changing in Memphis. On April 4, 1968, Martin Luther King, Jr. was assassinated. Memphis had become a city of unrest. The uncertainties in the city's climate were obvious, especially in the music industry. For Allen Reynolds, he felt as though he needed to look elsewhere. So, Allen headed for Nashville where he already had some music connections.

Jack "Cowboy" Clement was a "right hand man" to Sam Phillips. He was actually the man that discovered Jerry Lee Lewis. He was a great producer and songwriter. Jerry Lee did a song that Jack wrote called "It'll Be Me." Jack had the unique ability to hear a good song and put a good sound with it. After all, he learned from the greatest—Sam Phillips.

Jack and Allen had become friends by this time. Jack was always helping people get started in the music business, especially if they had talent—and he saw talent in Allen. Jack was good at doing things differently, whether it was writing or producing, and had a close relationship with Allen and Dickey Lee. Needless to say, Allen quit the banking business and devoted himself full-time to writing and producing.

Reynolds says, "This was not that big of a shift for me. I had been doing this for some time. Sometimes I would work at the bank and then be in the studio until three or four o'clock in the morning. This is just what I always wanted to do."

Once Allen arrived in Nashville, he was another voice that encouraged Bobby to move to Nashville. In fact, Allen once told Bobby, "Man, you need to move up here to Nashville. Memphis has slowed down, and Nashville needs your kind of playing."

By the time Bobby moved to Nashville, Allen was working with Crystal Gayle and others. Bobby played on a lot of her records. Allen and Bobby worked with Crystal for approximately nine years, including some of the writing. One of the biggest hits Crystal had was "Talkin' in Your Sleep" written by Bobby Wood and Roger Cook. It won the Burton Award for that year and was the most performed BMI song in the year it was released.

After working so close with Bobby on several projects, Reynolds said, "I don't know of anyone that knows more about making a great record than Bobby does."

Bobby, Dickey, Allen and Knox Phillips produced a top twenty record for a group called "Smoke Ring." The record was "No Not Much." Allen went on to produce and write songs for Don Williams, Crystal Gayle, Kathy Mattea, Hal Ketchum, and the legendary Garth Brooks, just to name a few. Jack built several studios and produced Don Williams, Charley Pride, and many, many more.

Bobby had yet another contact in the music industry. He knew that Allen Reynolds was talented and would be an individual that had his pulse on the music industry. He ended up playing on some of the demos for Jack, Allen, and Dickey.

Allen also recognized Bobby's unique talent as a writer, producer, and studio musician. Allen often tapped Bobby when he needed that special touch or direction for different artists. Bobby worked a lot with Allen and built not only a working relationship, but also a strong friendship.

Dickey Lee and Bobby became great friends when Dickey was putting his songs down on demos back in the Echo Studio days in Memphis. Dickey had a big hit while he lived in Memphis. "Patches" was a number one record and is still remembered today as a smash record of its decade.

People in Memphis tended to become jealous over those who had number-one hits. Snide comments would be made to the artist about the song. After "Patches" had been out of the charts for some time, a guy walked up to Dickey and asked, "How does it feel to be a has-been?"

Dickey replied, "Better than a never-was!"

Bobby said, "Way to go, Dickey!"

After his move to Nashville, Bobby discovered that Memphis was a very negative town during those days. More often than not your ideas weren't very positively received. You would often hear why things wouldn't work instead of how it could work.

Bobby learned that when you are in the studio creating music for the song, it is much like your first-born child coming into the world. It is like Picasso painting a beautiful picture and you are allowed to create part of that picture. You are adding the colors to the canvas. One fact remains true. Regardless of where you are, whether it's Memphis or Nashville, or any other recording city, the thread of creativity will always be the common ground.

Bobby always felt humbled and blessed to play such a part in the recording industry for over fifty years.

# *Chapter Fifteen*

### It's Time to Move

Johnny Christopher began working at different times at American Studio. His acoustic guitar rhythm was impeccable. His sense of rhythm was superb. By the seventies he played on most of the sessions. Reggie Young welcomed the acoustic rhythm because that freed him to just play electric guitar. Johnny played on several hits including those of B.J. Thomas and many others. He wrote "Mama Liked the Roses" that was recorded by Elvis Presley. It was during this time that Johnny and Bobby became very close friends. After Bobby moved to Nashville, Johnny began to be on the musician's first call list.

In the latter part of 1971, Johnny Christopher and Bobby went to the studio just as they did every day at noon. Most of the accounts had stopped coming to American. Atlantic Records had tried to hire the band to move to New York. At the time they did not know what had happened but thought that Atlantic had been blocked out and were not invited back. Atlantic wanted to know what it would take for the band to move to New York. Of course, at that time, no one wanted to go to New York. When the labels stopped coming in, Chips and the band started their own label. Hindsight told them that was the wrong thing to do. They didn't have any artists; they didn't have any songs—they didn't have anything. And with nothing in play, they weren't making any money.

If this was not bad enough, the rule was that if you worked at another studio while you were working for American Studio, you would be fired. That was constantly hanging over their heads. This was a topic of constant conversation for Johnny and Bobby. Actually, they were trying to get up enough nerve to leave.

One day they both arose and had the same idea. They headed to Nashville to explore "Music City" possibilities. One of the first people they saw was Tommy Cogbill. Tommy's initial reaction was one of surprise.

He looked at the Memphis twosome and said, "Don't ya'll tell anyone that I am here." Bobby and Johnny agreed. And they had a request of their own. They looked at Tommy empathetically and said, "Well, don't tell anybody you saw us here either."

Bobby and Johnny spent the day looking at the Nashville scene. Bobby knew Scotty Moore and had talked to him. Scotty had told Bobby for a long time that he could make a lot of money in Nashville. As the day went on, they met people with open arms—people like Buddy Killen and Fred Foster. Allen Reynolds had conveyed the message of work and success in the Nashville music scene. They were told that they could keep the work flowing. Bobby and Johnny were told that they could literally work around the clock.

Bobby knew without any uncertainty that it was time to move from Memphis to Nashville. He could not curtail his enthusiasm. Bobby and Johnny jumped in the car and headed back to Memphis. Those were the days of the CB radio. Bobby had a radio in his car and another CB radio at his house. He was able to keep in close contact with family and they would always know where he was.

He got Janice on the CB radio and told her, "We are on our way back to Memphis. Start packing! We are moving to Nashville." Janice's initial response was, "You're kidding me!" Bobby told her, "Hey, we can starve in Nashville as well as we can starve in Memphis."

Bobby got home and the packing began. Bobby and Janice's house went on the market immediately. At the same time, they were looking for a house in the Nashville area. They moved to Nashville in March of 1972.

During the transition from Memphis to Nashville, Bobby had to tell Chips of his plan. When Bobby called him, Bobby got the reaction that he expected but wasn't really prepared to deal with at the time. Chips began to tell Bobby, "You can't leave me. You're going to ruin everything. We're just beginning to get rolling here with our own label. Man, you're really letting me down."

Chips told Bobby to think about his decision for a few days. Bobby agreed to do that but even in agreeing he hated himself for telling Chips that he would think about it. Bobby knew even then that it was over in Memphis. He knew that he wanted to move on to the next chapter in his career, but at the same time Bobby hated to hurt Chips.

Bobby thought about this for hours and finally picked up the phone to make that dreaded phone call. He told Chips that he was moving, that this was something that he had always wanted to do. The decision was made and the direction was clear.

Bobby and Janice moved and never looked back. They found a house in the middle of Brentwood, Tennessee, that had an acre of ground with it. The scary part had just begun. How were they going to pay monthly notes on this house? How would they support themselves? They purchased their Nashville home for $41,000 with a house payment of four hundred dollars per month. This move was a move of blind faith, but now had a large debt tied to it. But Bobby had an inner peace—a peace that came from knowing that this was absolutely the right thing to do.

The sessions in Nashville were strictly union three-hour sessions. If you went over by five minutes, you were paid overtime. At first Bobby didn't feel like he was doing anything at all. If he worked two sessions in a day he would be home by six o'clock, compared to the long hours that he was used to at American.

No looking back. It didn't take long to confirm that Nashville was where Bobby belonged. He more than doubled his years in Memphis during his first year in Nashville.

# Chapter Sixteen

A Band Connection

Bobby was already becoming established in Nashville. His name was becoming a known entity in music circles. Johnny Christopher, Tommy Cogbill, and Bobby had made the move to Nashville. The work was literally pouring in at the time. In early 1972, when the rest of the band left Memphis, they went to Atlanta with Chips. Six months later the remaining members of the band, along with Chips, made their move to Nashville.

Bobby Emmons stopped by Bobby's house to talk about working together in Nashville. Bobby told his friends, "Man, you know, I can hook ya'll up with all of the sessions you want." Everybody was getting on board.

Not long after that, they started working four sessions a day with work often extending from the weekday into the weekend. It came to a point where they were working all masters. In fact, they were working so many masters that they could not take any demos. They were also cutting rhythm and blues, pop, and country.

Things were popping up all over the place. One of the early sessions was Kris Kristofferson singing "Why Me, Lord" for Fred Foster. Then there was Joe Tex. Buddy Killen did "I Gotcha." Some time later Chips brought in B.J. Thomas and he recorded "Somebody Done Somebody Wrong Song." Chip Young hired the group to record "I Can Help" with Billy Swan. Things just did not seem like they could get any better. Chips eventually built a studio in Nashville. It was located at Eleven-Eleven Seventeenth Avenue, and he named the studio Eleven-Eleven.

The band was cohesive. This band has always been special—they have a special chemistry and a special sound. But even in the music business there is the "A" group—those people who have been around the music circles forever. Often times some or all of the Memphis guys would record three or four songs on an artist only to have the Nashville A-team crew finish the album.

The Memphis band had a sound like no other, but there were only three producers in Nashville that would use the band as a unit. Most of the time the producers hired the band members individually. They would instruct their staff to "hire one of the Memphis Boys." That's how the name finally came into play. These guys who moved to Nashville from Memphis were forever named "The Memphis Boys."

Bobby and Johnny Christopher spent a lot of time together when they weren't working. Bobby had always admired songwriters, and Nashville was a writer's town. Bobby and Johnny would write until the wee hours of the morning.

In 1975, Bobby met a guy from London, England. Roger Cook was a mega pop songwriter. He had major hits in Europe. Some of his hits included, "I'd Like to Teach the World to Sing," "Long Cool Woman in a Black Dress," and "You've Got Your Troubles."

Roger came up with the idea to form a company that would distribute the music from publishing companies around the world. Picalic was formed in 1975. Roger, Bobby Wood, Ralph Murphy and Charles Cochran would be the writers. They each had their own publishing specialty. Ralph would be the one designated to make deals with foreign sub-publishers around the world for each of their companies. They started immediately and overnight it was instantaneous success. This went on for fourteen years. There were hits all over the world.

The group found out they could get money from sub-publishers; they were the first in Nashville to start that. There was a lot of success from Picalic. Roger and Bobby had written "Talking in Your Sleep," and "What's Your Name, What's Your Number." Ralph and Bobby had written "Half the Way" and "He Got You."

There were other hits out of the company. Writers would be signed. People like Roger and Sam Hogin who wrote "I Believe in Love, I Believe in You" by Don Williams. Then there was "Love Is On A Roll." There were major producers and artists coming by, including Chet Atkins and Crystal Gayle. They attracted producers and others connected with the Nashville music industry.

People were coming by the office and listening to songs because Picalic had become one of the most popular companies for songs. Most of the writers at Picalic wrote songs, but they didn't write straight country, so the people connecting with Picalic were getting not only number-one country records, they would cross over to the pop charts, too.

People wanted to be a part of what they knew would be music history. They wanted to be a part of success. The group celebrated. Soon they were dubbed with having the biggest Christmas party in Nashville. The parties went on for twelve to thirteen years. The last Christmas party cost approximately $35,000. They continued to party, blow money, and just live it up in the biggest way.

But the riding high was soon to come to a screeching halt.

Soon things got out of control and the company started going down hill. The new bank owners called in the loan, and the company had to be dissolved. This was a huge blow to everyone involved, but in 1980 Bobby began to get his life back on track. The party life was not a lifestyle that suited Bobby's upbringing and family values, so he knew that he needed and wanted to reconnect spiritually. He had begun to lose his soul, his direction, and his purpose in life. He wanted success. But the success he sought was with the Lord and not with man. So, once Bobby made that spiritual recommitment in his life, he began to see blessings flow in other areas as well. Once again, he found that purpose, not only in his spiritual life, but also in his music life. He had been making choices—choices that did not please God or give him the inner peace that he sought to have. He made a conscious decision to put God first, and he began to see the richness of God's blessings from that decision.

# *Chapter Seventeen*

### Days with Garth Brooks

Bobby always stayed connected with his Memphis and Nashville friends and had always maintained his relationship with Allen Reynolds. After all, Allen was a good friend and was brilliant in the music industry. Allen had been working with Kathy Mattea from the beginning of her career and he knew that Kathy's career had good legs under it and that she was pretty well established in her career.

In a late night conversation with his engineer, Allen said, "I would love to find a guy to work with, someone that I have had as much fun with as I have had with Kathy."

About three to four weeks later, Allen received a call from Bob Doyle, who was managing Garth Brooks. Allen and Bob had met but did not know each other well. Bob had worked at ASCAP when he and Allen had once crossed paths. Bob placed a call to Allen and told him he was working with a singer that he wanted Allen to hear. At that time Allen said to Bob, "Well, I am not looking but I am open to hearing him."

Garth Brooks attended Oklahoma State University in Stillwater, Oklahoma. While in college he began to play the guitar and sing. Even then he was beginning to develop a deeper interest in music. Garth graduated in December, 1984 with a degree in advertising. He came to Nashville with a "winner" attitude and demonstrated from the beginning that he was willing to take chances and to step outside of the box.

Bob and Allen got together and listened to some tapes that Garth had made and Allen instantly liked what he heard. In fact, he liked it so much that he suggested that Bob and Garth get with him to talk about Garth and his future in music. Allen used the same approach with Garth that he had used with every other artist.

Reynolds stated, "I like to get together with an artist and interview them and let them interview me. You may like an artist but you may not work with them that well. If, after talking for a while, it feels pretty good, then I suggest that we do a couple of recording sessions together—that we find some songs that we both love and go in and see how it goes." Continuing, Reynolds said, "Garth, if you're game we'll go in and do that and if feels good to us we'll go forward. If it doesn't then all either one of us has to say is hey, I love you but I don't think that I am the right guy."

Deciding to move forward, Allen and Garth began discussions on who should be in the band.

Allen asked Garth, "Are there any musicians that you have worked with that you have particularly liked and would want to have?"

Garth's response was brief because his experience in Nashville was limited at that time. He said, "No, not really. I can only think of one and that's Mike Chapman who is a bass player."

Allen agreed that Mike would be a great addition to a band for Garth but also knew a drummer that grew up with Mike and felt they would compliment each other very well. His name was Milton Sledge.

One day Bobby dropped in to talk to Allen at his studio and found Allen and Bob Doyle standing outside talking. They asked Bobby if he would come in and do a spec session for a guy that he had found just to see if they could find a direction for him. Bobby said, "Sure, I'll do it." Bobby was always willing to help people, especially the new artists. In fact, he would often do freebies for people just to help get them going. Allen set up the session.

Allen Reynolds put a group together that consisted of Bobby Wood (Keyboards), Chris Leuzinger (Electric Guitar), Milton Sledge (Drums), Mike Chapman (Bass), and Mark Casstevens (Acoustic Guitar). For the overdubs they added Rob Hajacos (Fiddle) and Bruce Bouton (Steel Guitar). They were later as referred to as "The Magnificent Seven" or even more commonly known as "The 'G' Men."

Allen would later say, "These guys knew how to put it in the pocket. They could just make it happen. And there was a bond between them that is unmatched by other bands."

There were some songs that had already been chosen. Allen and Bobby had a discussion before the first session began. They talked about a direction for the band tracks. Allen didn't think the typical Nashville direction would be right for Garth, so Bobby suggested taking the tracks about half way to Memphis, funk it up with a little soul. That's the direction that was taken on the first three songs. "Much Too Young," "Not Counting You," and "I Know One" became initial cuts and a couple of number-one records the first day.

When Bobby first met Garth in August, 1988, he saw a simple, humble guy from Oklahoma. But behind the personality was a drive and a willing spirit to do whatever it took to become a successful recording artist. When Garth extended his hand to Bobby, what Bobby saw was a sincerity that he had not seen in a long, long time. This guy from Oklahoma had a story to tell in his music.

During the time of putting Garth's songs together, a national TV show was being recorded in Nashville. The station called Bob Doyle and wanted to know if he had anybody they could use for the program. The TV show had a last minute cancellation and needed to fill the slot. Since this was a last minute request, some of the band members had previous bookings and were not able to be present. However, most of the band went along with Garth and performed on the TV show. Garth did two of his songs that had been cut.

Shortly after that, the switchboard lit up. Things just started snowballing. Teenagers, young kids, adults—people of all ages were hooked on the Garth Brooks' phenomenon. What was the difference?

Bobby said, "I think it was mostly the sincerity of Garth believing the songs that he was singing." But the "feel-good" tracks combined with great vocals made the project rise to another level. Garth sang with the soul that Bobby had heard and talked about early in his own career.

Bobby developed an instant respect for Garth. In the early recording days, Bobby and Garth talked about other artists trying to sing a song, but for whatever reason they couldn't sing it with conviction. And no matter how great the song, without the conviction, the performance was just not there.

As time passed, Garth told Allen, "You know, before we ever started working together, when I imagined myself with a band on stage, I never imagined a piano player as a part of it. Now I can't imagine being without one."

Allen knew that these men were great as individual musicians, but there was no way to anticipate the sound that would come from the combination of talents from these men. Garth loved them all and loved the way they worked together. In fact, he never wanted to hire anyone else.

Allen explains it this way, "The guys in the studio have to hear it better than anyone else hears it. Their job is to make that recording so good that you want to hear it over and over, and that it's so good you want to go hear it live. But, the record that gets made in the studio is for all time."

He continues, "You don't have the advantage of the visual. That record from the studio has to be the one that wins your heart, just from hearing it. These studio musicians were just so good at that."

In one session, Mark Casstevens was not available and Allen had to hire another acoustic guitar player. Johnny Christopher was hired to play on "The Thunder Rolls." Johnny did a great job. Garth really liked Johnny's contribution to the session, but Garth wanted to keep his band in tact. To Garth, it just didn't feel right not having Mark Casstevens.

This band played soulful music. Their personalities fit with Garth's personality and their playing complimented each other. They made each other look and sound good.

Reynolds describes it this way, "When you go into the studio, you present a song to the musicians that they have never heard, and within a three-hour session you take that song and work out a total arrangement and record it. It becomes the basic record from scratch. It takes a real collaboration between everybody. This band always had an unusual rapport. We never threw a song at them that they didn't just knock it out of the ballpark."

So what was it like to work with Garth Brooks in the studio? Every musician has his own story. If you ask Bruce Bouton, he will tell you, "I ended up overdubbing on a lot of stuff. There were a lot of great moments where we did things as a band, but I remember sitting in that studio and hearing Garth say he had a song. We never worked with a demo. Garth might come in with just an acoustic, and we would just make stuff up."

Bouton continues, "I remember one night we had about ten minutes left in the studio. Garth had a song that he and Kim Williams had written. He started playing this little rhythm thing to "Papa Loves Mama." Mark Casstevens starts this cool guitar lick and Bobby got on the Wurlitzer and started chugging on this thing. Rob came in and started playing on this. About that time somebody came into the studio and said, 'Hit the record button.' That song was cut on the first take." That song just had a "click" to it. It worked from the beginning. But there were other songs that fell into that "click" category—songs like "Rodeo," "Ain't Goin' Down Till the Sun Comes Up," "Standing Outside the Fire," "We Shall Be Free," and some of those real up tempo songs.

The ballads were stories unfolding in music that were embraced from the first word and the first note.

Chris Leuzinger says, "When Bobby was on a track, I think Allen felt comfortable. Allen was always listening to the song, but he was listening to the feel of that song. I think that Bobby was part of Allen's foundation because Bobby was just the kind of guy that could feel the song. Allen knew that." "I remember the song, 'The Thunder Rolls.' At the end of the first section and the beginning of the turnaround, there is a low chime or orchestra bell that Bobby played. Again, it was just one ring or toll, but I can't imagine the song without it. Bobby's part sends shivers down my spine every time I hear it."

Milton Sledge describes the group this way, "Individually, everybody is good, but together it becomes something really great. We have different influences coming together from all over the southeast. When we mixed that with Garth's influence from what I would call the west (Oklahoma) and the sound of rock, you mix it together, all of the best starts to come out."

Mark Casstevens explains, "When we are not doing this, we are all pretty much doing the same thing. We go out and play recording sessions with other random studio bands. There is a vibe on every session, and it is dictated by the personalities on the session. That affects how you play, whether you want to play, whether you want to suggest something, and unfortunately there are usually one or two alpha dogs that will take that vibe and diminish it."

He goes on to say, "With this group, the ego level of this group is healthy. Everyone had his ego in check from the top down. From Garth down to every musician, egos were not an issue. In fact, Garth called everyone 'boss.' And he's the boss! But it's that vibe—the one that shows no one has anything to prove and to do anything other than make a good record. It's one reason I always enjoyed coming to work here. I knew that it would be a mellow vibe and no one would step on someone else's territory. Anybody that has an idea gets it auditioned."

Getting the "G" Men together gives you an opportunity to see the magnificent talent and magic of seven men who are extraordinary.

To hear Mark tell it, "Everybody here has driven up to a session and seen a certain car and have thoughts of *do I have to work with these people?* You drive up to one of Garth's sessions and see the cars and just think *yeah this will be good*."

Bobby shared some of his earlier experiences with Garth. The band in Memphis would work with an artist until they finally had a hit. Then you would never hear from them again—one-hit wonders! That always nagged at Bobby's way of thinking. Why would an artist want to go in a different direction when they had something that worked! Live by the old theory that when you find something that works, don't mess with it. Don't mess with it at all! When it works, it works! Whatever you've got going—"if it ain't broke, don't fix it!"

From the start, Garth held on to his own individual style. He has always been extremely loyal, giving, honest, and up front, but most of all, he was honest with his music.

Garth gave his best in his recording sessions. Rob Hajacos says, "If you played hard, Garth wanted you to play harder. If you played loud, Garth wanted you to play louder. We would work so hard that it was absolutely draining, but it was draining in a really good way because you always knew that you were going to be well represented—by Garth, by Allen, and by this group of musicians."

Rob continued, "As the years have gone on, we have had a greater appreciation for each other. We miss each other because we don't see each other as much as we used to, and it was always a joy to get together."

The first time Bobby heard the song "If Tomorrow Never Comes" he asked, "Who wrote that song?"

Garth replied, "I did along with Kent Blazey." Bobby responded, "Wow, what a great song!" At that point Bobby recognized that Garth's talent went far beyond his singing; he also saw his ability as a brilliant songwriter.

Working in the studio was an unbelievable experience. As the musicians relate, "Garth always came into the studio with a joke. He came in and gave the band members those great big old hugs, told a couple of jokes, and turned it into more of a hang time than a serious recording session. He's always in a good mood."

To quote seven band members, "Garth is a heck of a guy. Most of the songs we cut, Garth borrowed Mark's guitar and sat down in the middle of us and played the song. He had lived with the song so much that he had learned how to play it. Many times, the only time we would hear the song was when he sat down and played for us on the guitar. He was amazing!"

Mark said, "Garth came into the studio and he had done his homework. When he came in and did the song, he had done the song several different ways and had thought through and twisted it around several different ways. He had a great ear and most people don't realize what a great musician he really is."

To further understand the "magic," you had to know that Garth was not judgmental and neither were any of the other guys. People were accepted for who they were and what they could contribute. Garth always tried to uplift everyone.

Rob explained, "Garth had the coolest, most diplomatic way about coming into the studio. He made you feel good about yourself."

The mood was set by Garth's light-hearted attitude with all of the guys. He made it easy for them to work and contribute. They bonded as friends and co-workers. When it was time to record, it was effortless to get the session cut.

Bobby will tell you that Garth always has been a super giving person. Very often there would be a need for Bobby to come to the studio to do a B3 organ overdub. Usually, Bobby would not be in the studio more than 30 minutes. Garth would want Bobby to sign a card for pay, but Bobby would decline to sign the card.

Bobby believes that everyone in this industry needs to give something back no matter how small it might seem. Bobby said, "If you don't give something back to your business, before long there will be no business."

He wanted to invest in what he had been blessed with for so many years—he felt like it wasn't right or necessary to charge for such a minimal amount of work. But most of the time Garth would end up putting Bobby's name on the card anyway.

Bobby and Garth have always had a great rapport. Since Allen Reynolds had shared Bobby's success with Garth, Garth wanted to know how things were done during Bobby's recording days in Memphis.

Bobby explained the difference between recording in Memphis and recording in Nashville. When he first came to Nashville he did four songs a session, which amounts to four songs in three hours. Most country songs will let you do that because the country format is much simpler than the pop format. Country has a much more narrow set of rules and you can't go too far from those boundaries. It's more lyrical and less musical than pop. A pop format requires more time to find a direction for the song as well as the artist. Most of the time it can't be done in three hours.

If you want something extra, it is going to take you longer. Often, musicians and artists would work at least half a day or longer on one song—working until it was right. When the bed tracks are completed, then the overdubbing process begins. This process can last for days or until you are satisfied with the final product, which is what makes a record stand out from all the rest.

This was another of the jewels that Garth used. He began taking more time with the songs. Garth would do a song—but only if he could believe what he was singing.

One vivid picture came from a movie. Garth and the band were in the studio for a recording session. Garth walked over to the piano and asked Bobby, "Do you remember a movie called *The Man from Snowy River*?"

Bobby replied, "I just watched it again a couple of weeks ago." Garth began to relate a scene from the movie.

He asked, "Do you remember the scene where the horses were running through the water? It was in slow motion. The pebbles were coming up around the horses' faces."

Bobby responded, "Yes, very vividly. I remember that scene."

Garth looked at Bobby and said, "With that in mind, play an intro to this song." And with that picture in Bobby's mind, he looked at Mark Miller and asked him to turn on the tape machine. Bobby could hear the notes in his mind and feel the music in his soul. He began to play an intro to what would become "The Dance."

As Allen Reynolds listened he said, "I had goose bumps! That song just came together, Bobby's intro just set the tone for that cut that we did."

Mike Chapman remembers recording "The Dance." He says, "Bobby just took off on that intro after a brief conversation with Garth. Just like that, Bobby had it. It's that beautiful thing that we all know. I was like, WOW, where did that come from? Bobby just created that on the spot, just like that! It just blew me away that he was so creative and so quickly. I can't imagine the song without that 'intro' and 'outro' playing."

Milton Sledge said, "When I heard Bobby start that piece on 'The Dance,' I thought what in the heck am I going to add to that? I was sitting on that drum stool and I was amazed!"

Sledge went to Allen and Garth and said, "I feel like if I add drums I am going to be in the way. To me less is more and that's just way too cool for a bunch of banging drums."

Allen and Garth both agreed and told Milton to sit out for a little bit. Milton went into the control room and as he listened he realized he could play lightly on that track. But the intro to that song gave the song recognizable character. It had Bobby Wood's signature on it.

For the band, their relationship is cemented with respect and sealed with talent. Milton Sledge states, "Bobby is by far one of my favorite piano players in this town. And not only that, he can play electric piano, a great B3, and he has the sensibility to play just what is needed. That puts him miles ahead of most anybody that I can think of."

Rob Hajacos adds, "Bobby is just really musical. He is always listening to what is going on around him. We are not technicians. We play from the school of hard knocks. This band is always listening to each other." Rob continues, "I knew who Bobby Wood was long before I played with him. To get the opportunity to not only work with him but to become his friend is pretty amazing."

Hajacos tells some incredible moments in the studio. He remembers one recording session where a ballad was being recorded. As he shared, "Bobby stood up, leaned over into the piano and laid his hand down on the strings that he was going to play to mute. I had never seen anybody do that before. What he did made sense and to me, it was just really, really cool. I have never seen anybody do that before or since then except for Bobby."

Chris Leuzinger and Bobby had worked with Bobby since the late 1970's. They had worked on some of Crystal Gayle's songs together. To hear Chris talk about their long history as musical partners, he will tell you, "Listening to Bobby play is just incredible. His timing on a session is unbelievable. He's like a rock. He's solid. Bobby could drive it home. If he got into a certain rhythm feel I could just jump on top of it."

For some of the band members, Garth's artistry and stardom just snuck up on him to some extent. His approach was subtle, and he was so gracious about the way he handled himself.

"All of a sudden we realized we were two or three albums into a superstar's career," says Hajacos. Mark Casstevens adds, "The sales on 'No Fences' was jaw-dropping. We knew then that whatever he was going to record, people were going to buy it. To me that was a little bit of odd pressure because you wanted to please him and you wanted to make the greatest record because you knew that it was going to get heard by lots of people."

"The Dance" was a monster hit. It was followed by "Friends In Low Places." At that point, the band members all knew that they were a part of music history and Garth Brooks was a superstar.

Chris remembers that as the group played together more and more there were some luxuries that were afforded to the band. "Once Garth became more successful, there was the lack of the clock ticking as far as developing arrangements and things like that," says Chris. He further stated, "With Garth, it got to where we were able to spend as much time as we needed to get the track done. After that, we could go in individually, listen to our part, scope it out, and make it right."

"If we got to a bridge and three or four people had an idea, we all had a chance to have our ideas heard and we came up with what we all thought was the best idea," he said.

The musicians all agree that there was never a "showboat" thing—no one ever worked to make sure they had their part on there. It was always about the song and what was going to make it work for the record and for Garth. But the one word that always popped up with the 'G' men was "magic."

What was it that made this whole experience magic? Bruce Bouton describes it like this, "Garth had this 'x-factor' that was evident from the beginning. There's never a period of time when Garth can't bring you to tears."

Mike Chapman adds, "Garth was unstoppable. It was great that we had a part in it."

But it was more than just what happened in the studio.

Rob Hajacos remembers, "I never walked out of the studio by myself. When I was here overdubbing, if I was the last guy to overdub at the end of the day, Garth always had something in his hand to help me to my car. He always made sure I was safely to my car. He would hug me goodbye and thank me for what I had done. That was the rule and not the exception. Many times that is when I would share personal conversations with him." Every band member has shared that same experience with Garth.

Rob further adds, "From the minute he opened his mouth we knew he was something special. But I don't think any of us ever saw coming what really happened. Things just started snowballing. Again, there is no pretentiousness and he is an unbelievable person to be around." But it went beyond talent. It went to connection and recognizing the potential in the star and the song.

Garth and Bobby have always been on the same page, which is a critical component; that's the key part of working with any artist. Garth once told Bobby that when he sings he sees pictures, he's acting out that song. Garth worked really hard to find his own special place as an artist and no one can deny that he has definitely made his special place in music history.

For Bobby, he never "just played on a session." He was often asked to play on a B3 organ or a synthesizer. He would be called back into the studio for additional sessions—just Bobby—because Allen knew that Bobby could add that "something extra" that would make the record special.

Garth would always have a lot of ideas about any given song. Garth and Bobby would work one-on-one on these sessions. Over and over Garth would ask Bobby to play something a certain way and Bobby would find a way to make it work. Garth had a vision and Bobby could share his vision. This further cemented their relationship.

Chris Luezinger explains, "Garth broke down the walls for other artists. He opened the doors for everybody." Garth Brooks did it right and it worked! This legendary music phenomenon is the top-selling solo artist of the twentieth century as reported by the Recording Industry Association of America (RIAA).

Garth and Bobby had the opportunity to collaborate in a writing venture. Together they wrote "In Another's Eyes." After writing the song, both agreed that the song needed to be sung as a duet. Garth suggested that Trisha Yearwood be the female artist.

'In Another's Eyes' was released as Trisha's first single on her new album, *Songbook*, and quickly went to number one. It was also put on Garth's next album, *Sevens*, which was another number one. Between Garth and Trisha, they ended up with approximately fifteen million in sales on those two albums.

Bobby recalls the first time that Garth truly acknowledged

the band. Garth had recognized and noted each of them on the CMA Awards as well as the ACM Awards when he won his first Album of the Year. Nobody does that. It's just the heart of Garth Brooks and who he is.

Bobby told Garth, "You are only the second artist that I have worked with in 40 years that has had this kind of heart and has taken care of us or done something above and beyond for the guys that worked with you."

Garth looked surprisingly at Bobby and asked, "Who was that other person?"

Bobby responded, "Elvis Presley. He would give you the shirt off his back."

Garth said, "Wow, I am in pretty good company."

"Yep, you are," Bobby replied.

Mark Casstevens sums it up this way, "Bobby is the senior member of this band. He's the oldest member of the group. I watched Bobby and was always interested in how he played. His note choice put less on the canvas so that when others come in and play the note he didn't play, it's not duplicated. It is done simply and tastefully. My thought is always how can I not mess up what he is doing. The keyboard and Bobby Wood drove a lot of those songs. I think that we all had the good sense to recognize that. That lends to good ingredients for a record—a good song done simply and tastefully. Bobby is able to do that."

Chris Leuzinger adds, "When Bobby plays, those melodic notes just flow out. 'Unanswered Prayer' is another example of simple but tasteful." Rob says, "Bobby always knew where to leave that space. The space he left was as important as the note he played. That's an inspiration to everyone. Bobby is the king of that. He installed a confidence in the group and set an attitude for us all."

To hear Bobby tell it, "I thought I was pretty lucky to have teamed up with the other members of the Memphis Boys. They became a second family to me. Then along came Garth Brooks and the opportunity to work with some really amazing guys—Garth and the 'G' Men. We spent a lot of time together and I felt like my family expanded even more. They are a remarkable group of people and even better friends."

Bobby has now worked with many, many artists. There have been a lot of legends. But two great legends have that first name recognition—Elvis and Garth. Bobby knew that he had walked in shoes that few, if any others, had ever walked before.

Garth Brooks has done it all. He has sold out the largest stadiums. He has sold millions and millions of albums. People know him by his first name. After a few years of retirement, he can still fill venues like no other. And Bobby Wood calls him his friend—an honor he doesn't take lightly.

## *Chapter Eighteen*

Getting the Right Sound

There's an art to playing on sessions, especially in deciding whether you play your instrument or whether you lay out. When the group was doing "I Can Help" on Billy Swan, Bobby Emmons brought a portable Wurlitzer, a raunchy little old organ out to Chip Young's studio in Murfreesboro. Billy had a song that he had written. So, Billy started playing the organ and singing. Most of Bobby's guys were playing on the session. Hayward Bishop was there with Reggie Young, Mike Leech, Bobby Emmons, and Bobby Wood. The studio was small and there wasn't much room. They were just going to put a track down with Billy playing the organ, drums, bass, and guitar. Of course, Bobby Emmons brought the organ so he was laying out, too.

When they got through putting that down, of course, they didn't have a solo or an intro on it. So, Chip Young tried to get Bobby Wood to go over and play a Fats Domino triplet on the piano.

Bobby said, "Man, man, man don't put that on there. That is

way too obvious to play on the piano. Why don't we do the triplets with sock cymbal or something small instead of the piano thing? Man, this thing doesn't need much. This is a number-one record here. It sounds different the way you've got it. Let's overdub some backgrounds and some tambourines and different kind of stuff and put it out."

Reggie went back and overdubbed an intro, and Chip Young overdubbed a solo on the guitar. They did some hollering and yelling on the end of it and hand claps. Sure enough, it was a number-one pop record.

Then it came time for a local banquet award program they had in town. Awards were given to musicians for playing on hit records. Well, one of the guys on the board was going to leave Bobby Emmons and Bobby Wood out. Chip Young really jumped up and down.

He said, "Let me tell you something, dude, Bobby Wood and Bobby Emmons' part on that record is louder than anybody else because they opted to lay out, which is kind of unheard of in Nashville. No, you are not going to leave them out. They did handclaps and different things. I know that there is no union scale for handclaps and things like that. They contributed to this record big time and they are going to get an award."

So he really stood up and said things were not going to be done typically by the union book. Things were going to be done right. Bobby Emmons and Bobby Wood ended up getting their awards.

Most of the musicians and producers knew that Bobby had moved to Nashville in the early 1970's. They had heard of the Memphis Boys and their special sound. George Jones and Tammy Wynette were getting ready to cut what would be their last album together called *Golden Rings*. The regular piano player was not available. Billy Sanford, a major guitar player in Nashville, told Billy Sherrill, the producer, "Man, these guys are in from Memphis. They are really great. The keyboard player is really super. He will do just fine on this."

And Sherrill said, "Well, call him!"

Sanford called Bobby Wood and that was one of Bobby's first big time Nashville sessions with the A-team. He was just learning to play the left hand of the piano with the bass player. They had a certain technique that was used to give a song that Nashville country sound.

Bobby remembers being scared to death. Bob Moore was at the left end of the piano with upright bass in a little booth. Buddy Harmon was right beside him playing drums. Billy Sanford, Grady Martin, Ray Eddinton, Pete Drake, Charlie McCoy, and the Jordanaires were there. It seemed like all of the Nashville rhythm section was there. Here was Bobby Wood, the only outsider playing on this session. He had his earphones on listening to George and Tammy singing and was trying to choke back the tears—thinking that this was fantastic. He was playing a different kind of music than he had ever played before, and he was playing with all of the guys that he had looked up to while growing up in the music world.

Buddy Killen would often use Bobby on his sessions— probably for fifteen or twenty years. They cut TG Shepherd, Joe Tex, Ronny McDowell, Bill Anderson and many more—anyone else he would bring in to produce. Buddy knew Bobby's rhythm and blues roots because Buddy had them, too.

Bobby's first introduction to Buddy was in Memphis when he brought Joe Tex in to record. The 827 Thomas Street Band had recorded several hits on Joe while they were in Memphis at American Studio. Buddy had come from Muscle Shoals, Alabama. He and Bobby had an instant connection, and Buddy came to rely on Bobby's ideas. So, Bobby ended up playing on most all of his sessions in those years between early 1970's through the 1990's.

## Chapter Nineteen

### Recognizing a Hit Song

Bobby was working non-stop. He was called into the studio to cut some songs on Kenny Rogers. Kenny Rogers' popularity was declining, his television show was off the air, and Larry Butler was trying to find him some songs to bring him back to the top again. The group was in the studio really late one night. Larry had pulled out a song called "Lucille." Kenny heard the song and immediately hated it. He really hated it. He just did not want to do it at all.

Reggie Young and Bobby were both on this session. It was coming up on midnight. Everyone wanted to go home. But Larry Butler just kept on twisting his arm wanting him to try this song. Bobby and Reggie heard it and knew that it would be a hit if Kenny would consent and just put himself into it. After much discussion, he finally did it.

They did one or two takes on that song. The rest of that was history too. "Lucille" was the single that launched Kenny Rogers into his second career.

When Herbie Mann came to American Studio, he brought four other jazz musicians with him including Roy Ayers, a bass player by the name of Miraslov, and two others. Bobby didn't have a clue what he would do on that album. The four guys that Herbie brought with him were class acts in the jazz field. They played more notes in one second than Bobby had ever played.

When Bobby figured out that the Memphis band was supposed to "do their thing" and let the jazz guys do theirs, it started to make more sense, and he became more at ease. Herbie wanted first takes on most everything. The band was definitely not used to that, but it all worked out in the end, and once again history was made.

In Nashville, Bobby had published his own songs for about twenty-five years. He decided to sign a publishing agreement with Bob Doyle and write for him for three years. During this time Garth and Bobby had written several songs including "In Another's Eyes." Bobby still had his own publishing company and continued to have songs released. Many of these were not country songs. Every time someone would release a song, it would usually cross over to the pop charts.

"Commitment" was a song written by Bobby during the time he was writing for Bob Doyle. Bobby had the title for this song for over a year. Every time he turned around, he would hear people talking about commitment—personal commitment to another person, to a cause, marriage—simple commitment. He had mentioned the title to writers in different writing sessions, but the title was all that Bobby had. At this point in time there was no music or lyrics to contribute.

Bobby filed this title away in the back of his mind. Charlie Monk was a major publisher in Nashville and had signed a new young writer. Charlie, a long time friend of Bobby's, called him one day and asked if he would write with this new writer. Once again Bobby saw the opportunity to help a young newcomer and so he agreed and booked a day to write.

On the morning of the writing session, Bobby was driving his usual route to Music Row. It was as though the music fell from the sky. Bobby had it —the music, the groove, and the chorus. When he arrived at the office, the chorus was written.

Bobby went into the office and introduced himself to this new writer. He sat down at the piano and began to play and sing the song. When Bobby finished he looked at the new, young writer and asked, "What do you think?" The guy looked at Bobby with an expression that said, "I don't have a clue."

About that time, Tony Colton, who usually showed up on the wrong day, came into the office. He thought he was writing with Bobby that day. Bobby played the portion of the song that he had written.

Tony listened and with amazement he looked at Bobby and said, "It's a smash! Put what you have on tape and hum the melody for the verse and the bridge." Bobby complied. Tony took the tape with him. He came back the next day and showed Bobby what he had. Bobby changed two lines and the song, "Commitment,"was complete.

Bobby and Tony put the song on tape and took it downstairs to play for the lady who worked in the front office. She used the same word that Tony had used earlier that same week—"Smash!"

Shortly after that they all went into the studio and made a demo to pitch. LeAnn Rimes' father, Wilbur, heard the song and took it to play for her. However, he did not put a hold on it. The next thing they knew, Wilbur called the office and said it was going to be her next single.

Within a short period of time, LeAnn was in the studio and recorded the song. Wilbur called the publishing office and said that LeAnn was performing the song on her shows and had a great reaction. It was her first release as a single from her album, *Sittin' on Top of the World*. It was a huge seller and immediately went to the top of the charts, selling in excess of one million.

On New Year's Eve in 1976, Roger Cook came to Bobby's house to write. After a time sitting around and kicking around some ideas, Bobby began to talk about situations that people love to hear. Things, like dreams and sleep, have always been mystical titles. Roger listened to Bobby and soon came up with the idea of "Talkin' in Your Sleep." With that in mind, Bobby sat there for a moment and started playing a melody. He began to sing a lyric of "three o'clock in the morning." That began to spark more lyrics from Bobby and Roger. They only had one verse and a chorus when they finished.

Later on, Bobby and Roger went into the studio and Bobby put the song down. It was just Bobby and the piano. He came in to listen to the playback. Roger used that word again—Smash! But he thought it was a smash on Bobby. They later called in a band and overdubbed to the track that Bobby had put down.

Roger and Charles Cochran got together and called seventeen string players into the studio and overdubbed them. Roger then took the finished product to a small label in Georgia. They paid him back for the cost of the demo and never sent a contract.

As time passed, Allen Reynolds heard the song and wanted to record it on the next Crystal Gayle album. Since Bobby was keyboard player on most of Crystal's projects, he was called in to play on her next album. The first song on that album to be recorded was "Talkin' in Your Sleep."

During that same period of time, Roy Day, a producer at RCA, had heard Bobby's version. He called the office and wanted to know if Bobby would consider having a single for RCA. He wanted to release the record just like it was. He said it was a hit song! RCA sent a contract and it looked like one volume of the encyclopedia. The contract had the same promotional language that Bobby had seen before. Bobby would be required to travel to radio stations and do "freebies." Now, he had been on that road before and did not want to travel it again. He immediately picked up the phone and called Allen Reynolds. Bobby asked him about the status on Crystal's album. Allen felt certain that "Talkin' in Your Sleep" would be the first single. Bobby then called Roy back and gave his appreciation and thanks for the offer. But his answer was "thanks" but "no thanks." He explained the scenario regarding Crystal as well as his own desire to stay off the road.

Crystal released "Talkin' in Your Sleep" in 1977. The song went to number one in the country charts and number twelve in the pop charts. Bobby knew that he made the right decision ,and the right person had released the song. Bobby and Roger received the Burton Award by Broadcast Music, Inc. (BMI) for the most performed (airplay) song of the year.

There are many examples of songs and how they came about, but there is one thing for certain—Bobby Wood knows a hit song when he hears it. It still goes back to his soulful roots.

# *Chapter Twenty*

A Friend for Life

Bobby had been on the Nashville scene for a couple of years when he met a woman by the name of Anita Moore. Anita went to work for Bobby at Picalic.

When Bobby first met Anita she was working with Jack "Cowboy" Clement. The pair became instant friends, and eventually, a brother and sister kind of team.

She worked with Allen Reynolds in his studio down at Jack's Tracks for a while. She was answering the phones and doing the book work. When Picalic was formed she found a new home. She handled most of the business for this new company.

When Picalic folded, Ted Hacker, a music artist manager, came over to Picalic. He wanted Anita to go into business with him. He had a place for her in management; she would be a full partner for the company that was being established, International Artist Management. Anita had made a good name for herself, and this was a great opportunity.

She told Ted, "I've got some baggage that I've got to bring

with me—wherever we go and whatever office we set up."

"What's that?" Ted asked.

She said, "Bobby Wood—I am not going to work anywhere without him. He is like a brother to me."

"That's fine."

And so, Anita and Bobby's partnership continued. Anita still takes care of Bobby's bookwork as well as the publishing end of his business.

Bobby led Anita to the Lord while he was at Picalic. Bobby knew Anita well enough to know that when she came in her office on Monday morning she would be hung over. She would have her doors closed.

Bobby was getting ready to leave one day, and he opened her door. He said, "Anita, I just wanted you to know that I love you and the Lord loves you, too." Then he just closed the door and left. Bobby found out a few days later that as soon as he closed the door Anita began to cry and could not stop.

A few days later, Anita cornered Bobby. They went into one of the offices and Anita said, "Bobby Wood, I know what you found is real. I've got to have it."

So Bobby led her to the Lord right there. Bobby told her, "You find a good church and get into the Word of God. You're going to find happiness that way. I made a decision a long time ago. If I never make another dime in this business, I am determined to be honest and to be happy. That's where I am."

Well, Anita made that decision and she's been in church ever since. She has raised two kids and sent them to a private Christian school. They have turned out to be fine, godly young people. And it all began with a life lived for the Lord.

Bobby and Anita have been the best of friends for many years. She tells people today, even her kids, that if they have any problems, then they should come and talk to Bobby. He will counsel with them and pray with them. He tells them that the Lord loves them and that He is their friend. He also makes certain that they know that he and Janice will be backing them in whatever they choose to do in life.

## *Chapter Twenty-One*

### The Lord Must Be First

During the mid-1970's, Bobby had gotten into drugs, booze, partying, and just plain wild living. It was around 1979 that Bobby became miserable in that condition. He had lost his creativity in his music. He was not living an honest life at home or at work. There was just an emptiness that he could not explain.

Don Schroeder and Tommy Cogbill had started going to a church in Brentwood. Bobby and Janice had been going to a different church. But the church was not meeting their needs. It was like going to a church building but leaving with an empty spirit. His life was spiraling downward.

Tommy was going to be baptized one night at a church called The Lord's Chapel. He had invited Bobby to attend the baptismal service. He agreed to go and witnessed his friend's baptism. Bobby had never even been in a church like this. It was called a full-gospel church. It was the first time in years that he had felt the presence of the Lord in such a powerful way.

Bobby and Janice started attending regularly. He said to

Janice, "I know this is not like where we are used to going." They really saw miracles happening and saw the Lord's hand at work.

Bobby was raised as a Baptist, and Janice had a Methodist background. To attend a full-gospel church was a totally different place for them spiritually. There was an excitement that neither of them had felt before.

This became the heart and soul of Bobby and Janice. They were growing spiritually in a way that they had never grown before. They could feel the presence of the Lord every time they were there.

The Lord's Chapel became their church home for the next twelve to thirteen years. The pastor, Billy Roy Moore, was a great Bible teacher. He taught through the Bible twelve to fifteen times within the period of time that they were there. Bobby credits his understanding of the Bible, his Christian walk, and his ability to minister to others to this significant chapter in his life.

After Bobby and his family had been at the Chapel for a few years, Bobby felt the calling to become a counselor, but he didn't know what to do about it. It just kept tugging at his spirit. One day the altar call asked for people to go upstairs for prayer relating to any needs that they might have. Bobby stopped one of the elders in the hallway and told him that he thought the Lord was leading him toward counseling. The elder opened his Bible and showed Bobby a piece of paper that he had written on just a few days before. The elder had been praying for counselors and the Holy Spirit had laid upon his heart. On that sheet of paper were the names of Bobby and Janice Wood.

Shortly thereafter, both Bobby and Janice went through the classes that helped them as they entered the ministry of counseling.

It was some time after that when Bobby was asked to visit the preacher in his office. Bobby had no idea what this man could possibly want with him. He began to wonder if he had done something wrong. When Bobby arrived, the pastor and the elders told Bobby that they wanted to recognize him as a deacon. They were all aware that he was doing the work of a deacon, and they wanted to pray over him and bless him as he served in that capacity.

Some time later, Bobby became an elder at the church.

A few days later, Bobby was working on his lawn tractor mowing the yard. While he was riding the John Deere, he was just singing and worshipping the Lord. As he prayed he asked the Lord, "What does it mean to be an elder—to serve you in this way?" Bobby was expecting to get an answer that was detailed and perhaps even mind-boggling. But his answer was simple and just one word—servant. It really put things in perspective. The Lord continued to speak to Bobby that day. And the more Bobby prayed, the more the Lord revealed Himself. Bobby began to cry "like a baby." Even today, when he feels his ego is getting in the way, he is reminded of that one simple word—servant.

Bobby played the piano and ministered to as many as he could. He and Janice ended up leading a lot of people to the Lord, praying for people that were sick, and seeing them get healed. Their faith was strong and sustained them. There was just no experience like that. And that experience has been the foundation of not only the present but also the future for Bobby and Janice.

## Chapter Twenty-Two

WHAT NEWCOMERS NEED TO KNOW

To this day, to the young writers that Bobby works with, those who are on the wrong path, Bobby will be more of a friend than anything. He will help them get started on the right road of being blessed and doing something major with their career. He will talk to them about not trying to be anyone but themselves and that they should always do their music honestly.

What is the most important message that Bobby has for these new, young writers? He tells them, "Don't copy anybody!" A lot of the music today has gone to computer music, but that computer music doesn't have a soul or feel to it. Record labels are folding. They are not making any money. It's just like the old saying, "You can fool some of the people some of the time, but you can't fool all of the people all of the time."

"Unless you do things that are honest in your music or whatever you do, then there can be no pride in what you are doing. Sam Phillips once said, "The day the dollar means more than the music then that's the day the music dies."

Bobby continues, "You have got to be happy with what you are doing. And to be happy with what you are doing, you have to be honest with it. And you have to give it your best. The great Creator that created everything is in us too. If I am not creating I am not really happy."

I think the Lord intended for us to let Him be part of our lives and to help us create, whatever line of work or profession we choose. When we get into a position to be creative, then I believe it will happen. I believe that it comes from the Almighty God that we serve."

When the Memphis Boys started traveling overseas playing for the Elvis fan clubs, they quickly found out that the fans dislike imitators as much as they do. The fans expect the artists to be different and to be original.

The music business is just like any other business. You have to work at it to be the best you can be. There are no "free lunches." Bobby will tell you, "There is no greater feeling in the world than to reach out and wait for the right thing to happen—just like 'The Dance.' The same thing goes for writing. Instead of just rhyming and putting something on paper, you have to wait for the great idea and wait for a great lyric, just like 'Commitment' and 'He Stopped Loving Her Today.'"

Bobby once read a statement from a 1930's composer who said, "I believe that all great ideas come to those who are in position to receive. I believe that all great ideas come from the heavens. I am at my keyboard at ten o'clock every morning in position to receive. I feel that if I am not in position to receive then someone else will receive the blessing." This thought has stayed with him and is one that he continues to live by every day.

Bobby has been called upon to counsel many young artists. Through the years he has found that anyone can be an average artist. The way to be different is to be yourself. There are so many copycat artists around; you can always find someone that is an imitator.

In today's music world, there are a lot of younger kids coming in who are trying to imitate Garth Brooks. Bobby tells them, "You need to pay attention to what Garth did and not what he sounds like. He dared to be different and think outside the box. But most of all, he stayed true to his own convictions."

Bobby remembers that very wise counsel from Sam Phillips. In the days when Bobby wanted to imitate Jerry Lee Lewis, he learned quickly that Jerry Lee was doing his own thing. But Bobby Wood had yet to arrive. No one will be a superstar unless they are true to themselves, thinking outside the box, and focusing on originality.

## Chapter Twenty-Three

DARKER DAYS—LONELY DAYS—WRONG CHOICES

In the normal sector of living it was easy to party, especially during the 1970's when Bobby first arrived in Nashville. Nashville was a party town for musicians. But the partying didn't just happen in homes—the studio lent itself to long days and even longer working sessions. During some sessions, there would be two tubs of beer iced down for the musicians and the artists. While it seemed fun, relaxing, and made everyone loose, hindsight taught one thing. Why would you want a bunch of drunk musicians on your session?

The ABC Paramount sessions would have about twenty people in the control room. The friends from the office would be there with bottles of wine. They would be drinking and offering wine to the musicians, and it would turn into a party. Some of the rock sessions would also have drugs and booze available for all of the musicians. Cocaine and marijuana were the biggest and hottest offerings at that time.

Marijuana was the drug of choice. It was readily available and was all over town. Sometimes marijuana purchases were made and sometimes people would share joints between songs.

Bobby had never seen marijuana before. Actually, he had never seen cocaine either. By the time everyone went home they were either intoxicated or high on drugs. It was only by the grace of God that the law did not stop anyone. How there were no accidents or incidents of jail time was nothing less than miraculous. In those early days you didn't dare say anything for fear of not fitting in. You didn't want to separate yourself from the rest of the group.

When Bobby first came to Nashville, a drummer for a rock star was in the studio for a session. He looked at Bobby and said, "Here, why don't you try this?"

Bobby asked him, "What is it?"

The drummer replied, "It is just something that picks you up and makes you feel good." Bobby didn't know what it was or what to do with it, so the drummer told Bobby what to do.

He took some himself and then told Bobby, "Just sniff it up your nose."

At first Bobby did not feel any different.

During a later session, another musician offered Bobby pharmaceutical cocaine. From his previous experience, Bobby knew what to do. He sniffed the cocaine. Soon after that he left to go home. On the drive home Bobby felt his throat begin to deaden. He couldn't feel himself swallow and pulled over to the side of the road, opened the car door, and began to vomit. Once he was over his feeling of sickness, Bobby closed the car door and drove home.

After a couple of months of use, Bobby became hooked on cocaine even though he did not recognize any addiction. Drugs were so readily accessible, especially on the rock sessions that it was just a matter of what to use and how you wanted to feel at that moment in time.

Side effects set in quickly. Bobby became paranoid. He was lying to his wife. It just began to eat him up on the inside. He asked God to help him kick this deadly, destructive habit. He did not know that there were others praying this same thing for him. Bobby had become hooked on a mind-altering drug, cocaine, but what he needed was a heart-altering relationship with Jesus Christ. He found that on those drives home after a session, he would be praying to God on one hand and high on the other hand. He had begun to hate himself.

Bobby knew the truth. After all, he had been raised in church. One night as he was driving home, he could only feel deep misery. As he was driving, he was on one of his cocaine highs. He was kicking himself and questioning why he had done that to himself. But the addiction was too great. When he got closer to home, he passed by the Lord's Chapel. That night he had a strong urgency to reach out to someone—to get some help. It just so happened that the mid-week service was in progress. Bobby parked his car, walked in and explained his predicament to first two men he saw. He told them the bold truth—"I need help." A couple of the church elders reached out to Bobby and began to pray with him. After the prayer time, Bobby felt relief, but the cocaine was still in his system.

Bobby felt like God was on one side and Satan was on the other, each one about to pull him into halves. He asked God to show him how to pray. By this time, he had quit the booze and marijuana but he was hooked on the cocaine. However, he finally quit buying it. But the temptation was still there. Almost any office that Bobby frequented would have cocaine on the desk along with a straw. The office staff would tell Bobby to "help himself and have a couple of lines." And that is what he did. He could pick up cocaine just like he would pick up a phone message.

Bobby was losing the one quality in music that he needed most—his creativity. He began to ask God to restore his creativity.

One day when Bobby was driving into town, he asked the Lord to show him how to pray. The Lord spoke clearly to Bobby and revealed to him, "Pray for the temptation to be taken away." For the next six months, these same offices had no signs of cocaine. By the end of those six months Bobby was free from his drug habit. God had truly answered Bobby's prayers.

Somewhere along the way, it was realized by studio executives that this actually did affect the quality of work and the end product. A decision was finally made that there would be no more drinking or drugs on any of the sessions.

Bobby quit the drugs cold turkey. He never went through withdrawal. He never looked back. God had delivered him from this destructive habit, and he knew that road would never be traveled again.

## Chapter Twenty-Four

Nashville Sound — Memphis Soul

It did not take Bobby long after he moved to Nashville to miss the way sessions were done in Memphis. He appreciated country music and the whole Nashville scene, but it could tend to get boring to do the three and four song sessions. While it had it's own niche, the opportunity to be creative or do something creative on a record seemed to have slipped away.

But he had developed a reputation for honesty in his music. Anyone working with him knew that Bobby had an ear for music like no one else.

One day Billy Sherrill was producing an album. The sound was good, but Bobby didn't feel anything to play. It was something for acoustic guitars and people telling stories, but there wasn't much melody to it.

Bobby went into the control room. He listened again. He said, "Man, I just don't hear piano on this."

Billy said to Bobby, "Get in here and sit down and help me produce this. I really appreciate the fact that somebody recognizes that his instrument doesn't need to be on a record. We've got enough people trying to please the producer and play to the producer rather than the song. I really do appreciate that."

That's just how Bobby Wood is. He is about the sound. He is about the record. He is about the soul of the music. That's why he has literally hundreds and hundreds of hits to his credit. The soul has never left him.

In the 1990s there was an opportunity that came from Allen Reynolds. He wanted the Memphis Boys, a.k.a. American Studio Band, to write some instrumentals and do an album with him as co-producers. There had not been instrumentals on the radio in years.

All the guys agreed that this would be something great to do—something different that no one else was doing. This project took two years to complete.

So, the guys all committed to the project. After two years of work, two of the songs ended up in the top-ten on the jazz charts. Sylvester Stallone heard the album and fell in love with the music. He was actually looking for a Memphis type of movie. Peter Jennings, the news anchorman, heard this album and told a friend that he loved to snow ski in Colorado and listen to the music. Some of the songs ended up as background music for soap operas.

Once again, Bobby Wood and the rest of the Memphis Boys found a new niche—true to who they were. They co-wrote all of the songs but still true to the soul of their music.

## Chapter Twenty-Five

MEMPHIS BOYS—WORLDWIDE FAME

The Memphis Boys had made a name for themselves in the music world. They had a sound that drew others to them. With the likes of Elvis Presley, Neil Diamond, Wilson Pickett, Dusty Springfield, B.J. Thomas, and many others having hits tied to this band, it was a wonder to many how they did it. What was it that made people want to record with this band and get a session scheduled with hopes of a hit record?

Gene Chrisman explained, "We played to the artist and we played to the song. We all listened to every idea. We had no bickering. We just got things done. We would change to make things fit to the song. We didn't play just to ourselves."

Bobby Emmons elaborated, "We were not a walking self-advertisement. We loved the music. We were not five one-band shows. We were all trying to work together to make it work."

While the Memphis Boys had established themselves as a premier band in the United States, there was yet another opportunity awaiting them. One of the guys got a call from a promoter in Belgium. He wanted to know what the chances would be of getting the Memphis Boys together and doing the songs on the two albums that they recorded with Elvis in 1969. He wanted them to entertain the different Elvis fan clubs in Holland and Belgium. Bobby was called to talk to the promoter and told him that the chances were good for a Memphis Boys show, but he had better "hurry up!" Bobby continued, "We are all on Social Security!" The promoter, Hubert Vindevogel, laughed hysterically.

That was their first venture of doing a Memphis Boys show or an American Sessions Band show for Elvis fan clubs over there. Of course, this was just the Elvis segment. But the Memphis Boys were there, and they packed out every venue.

European fans are different than those in the U.S. The European club members not only know the artist but they know every band member by name. They know who plays what instrument and what songs they had played on for every album.

Elvis had been gone for twenty-eight years. Bobby said, "They had never seen us or heard us play other than the records." They did one show in Belgium and one in Holland. Tickets were at a premium. Shows were sold out in a matter of hours.

It didn't take long for this to catch on like wildfire. Another promoter, Henrik Knudsen, from Denmark was coming through town. He and Bobby met at a restaurant in downtown Nashville. As they were talking, Henrik wanted to know if they had ever done a show in Memphis during Elvis week.

In their discussions, Bobby shared that the Memphis Boys had never been invited to participate in the Elvis tribute shows. Yet, two of the biggest albums that Elvis had were with the Memphis Boys—*Elvis In Memphis* and *Elvis Back In Memphis*."

Henrik asked Bobby, "What's the chance of us doing a show in Memphis on Elvis's 70th birthday?"

Bobby replied, "Well, probably good."

The show was booked. The Memphis Boys came home—back to Memphis—back to their roots. Along with them they had two background singers, Angel Smith and Cindy Walker. They hired three horn players from Memphis—the talented Jackie Thomas who had played on sessions at American. Along with Jackie were Scott Thompson and Jim Spake, two of Memphis' finest horn players. The two-night show was together, and the fans packed The New Daisy Theater in downtown Memphis.

People had traveled there from all over the world—Australia, London, Paris, and other parts of Europe. The word had gotten out that this was the show to see.

There was a lead singer that was going to do the show with them in Memphis. But the guy ended up on drugs. At the last minute the Memphis Boys found out that there were three singers from Scandinavia that were coming with Henrik.

Bobby called him and asked, "Do these guys know these songs?"

Henrik said, "Of course they do. They are great singers. All of them are artists."

Bobby said, "Let's get together and have a little rehearsal."

They came through Nashville a week before and had a rehearsal. Sure enough, they were really good singers. They were not Elvis impersonators, but were good singers that knew the Elvis songs. The show was a huge hit.

One of the performers was Bobo Moreno from Copenhagen, Denmark. He had a magical sound and the soul that the Memphis Boys had always loved. Bobo's performance was superb. In fact, the Memphis Boys would later bring Bobo to Nashville to cut four songs with him. These songs were placed on CDBaby.com. Bobby is currently pitching this project to record labels.

Bobby said, "Bobo is a name to watch. He is one talented performer. When the public hears him, they instantly love him. When he sings "As Long As You've Known Me," he captures his audience from the first note and carries them to the last with great soul."

Henrik could not have been more pleased. He also booked an eighteen-day Scandinavian tour in the Spring of 2005. Every single show was a sellout. People could not get enough of the Memphis Boys. An autograph session was set up after every show lasting two hours or longer each time. The press in Oslo, Norway, voted unanimously that the American Sessions band show was the "Show of the Year."

Europeans embrace the Memphis Boys like few others have ever seen. They cannot get enough of this soulful, classic music. These guys deliver from the first moment they step onto the stage until the last note is played. And the Europeans will stand in line until they get to shake the hand, get the autograph and take a picture with members of their favorite band.

# *Chapter Twenty-Six*

### Talking About the Hits

The Memphis Boys are five musicians who have traveled different roads but have the same destiny. They are recognized as music giants in their industry. Most of these guys are drawing Social Security. After the first New Daisy show, it was reported in a Memphis newspaper that these guys have been playing for fifty years, but they still sound like they did when they were twenty-five years old. They have a story for the world to see—a story for newcomers to hear.

And if you look at their numbers, you will see something phenomenal. They had twenty-three number one hits in Memphis and had one hundred twenty-three chart records on four different charts—from rhythm and blues to pop to country to jazz.

This is a part of the history of the Memphis Boys. It is a part of Bobby Wood's history. Bobby knew from the first moment that he set foot in Nashville that it was a songwriting town. When Bobby would drive to the nerve of Music City—downtown—he knew that there would be somebody to write with somewhere along the way.

One writer was a guy by the name of Johnny Christopher. In 1974 Bobby and Johnny got together at Stan Kesler's apartment. Bobby had a small Wurlitzer piano in there. Bobby had a rhythm idea that was going over and over in his mind. They sat down together andwrote a song called "Still Thinking About You." That was the first big song that Bobby had written. It was also his first number one.

Roger Cook and Bobby were writing hits like "Your Love Still Brings Me to My Knees," which has been cut in thirteen different languages. They also wrote "What's Your Name, What's Your Number," which was a big disco record for Andrea True and the Love Connection.

Somewhere along the way Ralph Murphy, one of the Picalic partners entered into the picture. He was a songwriter originally from Canada. Roger Cook wanted Ralph to write with Bobby. So, they sat down and wrote a song called "Half the Way." Crystal Gayle recorded the song and it soared to number one on the country charts and also went to number twelve on the pop charts.

Bobby and Crystal Gayle had a special relationship. They agreed on most everything when it came to recording. She had a special talent and was one of the easiest artists to work with in Nashville. At one point in time, Crystal wanted to do a gospel album. There was only one person she wanted to have produce it—Bobby Wood. The album, *Someday*, immediately caught on in the Christian circles and received a Grammy nomination.

Ralph and Bobby got together again and penned "He Got You." It was a number one hit for Ronnie Millsap.

Johnny Christopher and Bobby were still connected and got together to write "Better Love Next Time" recorded by Merle Haggard, which was another number one record for him. Bobby, Johnny, Reggie, and Mike also played on that session.

Whether it was writing a song, playing on a song, or both, there have been a number of hits throughout the years. There was "Mr. Bojangles" by Jerry Jeff Walker. There was also an artist who came in by the name of T.G. Sheppard. Bobby was a part of cutting his first number one hit called "Devil In A Bottle," which was produced by Don Crews. Don was a partner of Chips Moman during his days at American Studio in Memphis.

These songs coupled with songs like "Suspicious Minds," "In the Ghetto," "Kentucky Rain," "Sweet Caroline," and "Always On My Mind" will keep them in the forefront of the music industry for years to come. The list is too long to mention every song.

According to *Billboard* magazine, the Memphis Boys played on more hit recordings during a six-month period than any other studio rhythm section in history.

# Chapter Twenty-Seven

### Stars Past and Present

Bobby's hero early on was Jerry Lee Lewis. Stan Kesler was working with Jerry Lee. Bobby asked Stan if he could stay in the control room while Jerry Lee was recording. It was amazing for Bobby to see this legend at work. He found Jerry Lee to be cordial and still very talented. Bobby was in awe of the entire situation.

Bobby once found himself in a situation where an upright bass was needed on a song that he was getting ready to record. A guy walked in the studio. He looked like a vagrant with dirty overalls, a white tee shirt, a dirty cap, bathroom thong shoes—just a really unkempt looking individual. He looked like he could live on the street. He came in, spoke to Stan Kessler, and left. Bobby asked Stan, "Who was that?"

Stan replied, "That was Bill Black."

That was Bobby's introduction to Bill Black.

In working with Dusty Springfield, Bobby found her to be a person in awe of those who had come before her. When she came into the studio to record, she became speechless. She couldn't believe that she was standing behind the microphone where Wilson Pickett had once sung. In fact, Dusty returned to New York where her final vocals were later added to her recording.

When BJ Thomas came into the studio, Bobby was not originally overly excited. He knew he was good, but he just didn't know how good. They were there to record "Hooked On A Feeling," "Just Can't Help Believing," "Eyes of a New York Woman," and (later) "Somebody Done Somebody Wrong Song."

The Memphis Boys were involved in so many projects with so many starts that some of them did not always know when a number one hit was on the charts. There was no time to listen to the radio—just work and record—keep those hits coming.

Most nights Bobby would leave the studio during the wee hours of the morning, sometimes three or four o'clock in the morning. The last thing he wanted to hear was more music, so there was no radio on for the ride home. Records that were on the charts, records being played on the radio were pieces of information that he did not have.

Neil Diamond had recorded with the Memphis Boys. Wilson Pickett was working in the studio. The Box Tops came along and Bobby played on some of their later songs. A group that Chips had put together was Cymarron. They came in to record a song called "Rings." When Chips found the song, he put the group together and there was another top five record. The Memphis Boys were again the instruments behind the hit.

Dionne Warwick recorded 'You've Lost That Loving Feeling.' Bobby immediately recognized her amazing talent, especially because she always sang her own backup. She could perform in one take, and it would be perfect.

Bobby found Joe Tex to be one of his favorite early days singers. He had great talent, great personality and was amazing to work with in the studio. "Skinny Legs" and "I Gottcha" were cut in Memphis.

Danny O'Keefe had one hit with the Memphis Boys—"Good Time Charlie's Got the Blues." This was another case of the artist not liking the song, but the band knew that it was a hit. Merrilee Rush had one hit—a song called "Angel Of the Morning." Oscar Tony, Jr. recorded "For Your Precious Love."

Kris Kristofferson was an early introduction in Nashville for Bobby. His hit "Why Me, Lord" caught the attention of the public and again another hit was born. There was something else special about that song—Larry Gatlin and his family sang background.

At one point in time Merle Haggard offered Bobby the opportunity to work with him for his shows including Las Vegas. Every time Merle came to Nashville to record, Bobby got that call. Merle told Bobby that he was his all-time favorite piano player—he played with soul and had a unique sound that was considered out of the norm for the Nashville crowd. Merle didn't like the typical Nashville sound. He and most of the outlaws like Waylon Jennings wanted something different.

Bobby had already played with Merle on "That's the Way Love Goes," and "Better Love Next Time." Merle would often invite Bobby to his studio in California for recording sessions. In fact, Merle told Bobby that when he was not in the studio, he could come to wherever Merle was performing. Merle committed to renting Bobby a keyboard if Bobby would play his show, so Bobby took Merle up on his offer on a number of occasions.

Kathy Mattea came on the scene and worked with Bobby to record "Eighteen Wheels" and "Love at the Five and Dime," and "Going Gone." Emmy Lou Harris recorded "Thanks to You." Emmy Lou was tremendously talented and Bobby was delighted to work with her.

There were scores of other artists that came through the studio. But every artist knew that if they worked with Bobby or with the Memphis Boys then they would have the best of the best—the best chance for a number-one or chart-breaking hit.

Recently, Bobby was called and booked for another Garth Brooks project. When Bobby arrived at the studio, Garth told Bobby that he wanted him to meet someone. Garth turned around and said, "Bobby, meet Huey Lewis." Huey shook Bobby's hand and proceeded to tell Bobby that he had been filled in on all the mega hits that Bobby had played on over the years.

Bobby responded, "Man, you don't know this, but you are one of my all time favorite rock and roll artists. I love your records."

Garth, Huey, and Bobby got down to business and cut one of Huey's songs, "Workin' For A Livin." Bobby was grinning from ear to ear. He had just worked with another of his all time favorites. What a great job to have!

God always put Bobby in the right place at the right time. So many times Bobby has played on what would be the biggest hit a recording artist would ever have including Merle Haggard's "That's the Way Love Goes," George Jones' "He Stopped Loving Her Today," Kenny Rogers' "Lucille," Willie Nelson's "Always On My Mind," and the list goes on.

## Chapter Twenty-Eight

A Conversation with Bobby and T.G. Sheppard

One of the most rewarding times for musicians is a time to get together with friends past and present and talk about "old times"—times in the studio, recording sessions together, and just how things used to be compared to how they are now. Bobby and T. G. Sheppard had that kind of reunion and talked about fond memories.

"My career started walking the streets of Memphis looking for a break, walking into Sun Studio, knocking on doors, working with Roland James and Stan Kesler. Bobby's name has always been on the tip of my tongue since I have been in the music business. His career spans years and it is timeless...it just goes and goes," said T.G.

Bobby said, "I remember our first meeting at Phillips Studio. T.G. was putting his voice down on something, and I immediately recognized a special talent."

"My home was in Memphis. That's where I got to know Elvis really well. I basically lived at Graceland for seven years. I got to know George Klein and all of those people. I met Red West, Sonny West, and the rest of those guys. In fact, it was Elvis who bought me my first tour bus," said T.G.

Bobby replied, "When I worked with Elvis, I found him to be the same way. He was always such a generous person. He once offered me his ring, but I didn't take it. That's just how he was."

"I always just hung out. I knew of Bobby. I knew that he was playing on a lot of great records and knew he was considered a great musician."

"You were already in the record industry by then," said Bobby.

"Yes, I was in the record industry. I started off in the record industry at a small record company in the late 60's. I always wanted to be a singer. Then I left there and went to work for Stax Records. I was at Stax Records working for Al Bell and Jim Stewart for four years. That's where I became close with so many of the Stax Records stars like Al Green, Isaac Hayes, and so many others.

"I remember meeting you and really liking what we were going to do. I heard the song and knew it would be a hit," said Bobby.

"It was in the early 70's. I was sitting on the couch at the Ramada Inn in New York. It was a disc jockey convention. I was in the room with Waylon Jennings and his wife Jessie. I started singing, and Waylon wanted to know why I was in the record business. He said that I should be a country singer. Waylon gave me a red guitar and told me to take that guitar and go be a country singer. I went and became a country singer because Waylon Jennings told me to. In 1974 I went and cut my first country single, which was 'Devil In The Bottle.' Bobby was on it."

Bobby said, "It was in Nashville at Pete Drake's studio. It was a great record and a great session. It was a huge record; it was a number-one record right off the bat."

"It was the kind of record that you record on Tuesday, you

release on Wednesday, and it goes to number one on Thursday."

"It was a huge hit and it hit fast," said Bobby.

T.G. said, "It went to number one and stayed there for eight weeks. That was my start and that's when Bobby and I really connected. A lot of people say the drums hold the record together, but for me, the keyboard holds it all together. It is the only instrument that can give you the biggest sound.

"Some producers come in with everything in their mind, but the smart guys leave an envelope open for the musicians. You never know what is going to pop up and what you would have missed."

"You miss a lot with things that are so pre-programmed. My biggest records were the ones you guys played on where we just let you go. They actually get it together and that's what makes it work," said T.G. He continued, "The early days in Nashville were different than they are today. I remember at 5:00 in the afternoon you could get together with people and talk. People would be winding things down in their studio, and you could walk over and see what was going on across the street."

"Yea, and you could just sit around and joke with each other and laugh. We've lost that."

"Memphis had that at one time and when it went away, people started moving to Nashville," said T.G.

"I know and now we've lost so much of that in Nashville. We wrapped our music around the song and the artist."

T.G. said, "You always knew when you had magic back then. You could hear it! You could feel it. You knew when you had a hit!"

"I knew it on the first thing we did together. I thought what a song! What a performance! I really felt the soul in the performance."

T.G. replied. "I felt it, too. Bobby had lived up to his reputation, and I was really pleased with what we did. It just all came together and for me it happened so fast. I had several other number ones and Bobby was on them."

"Yea, it was a good blend. We had good material to work with and it just all came together the right way. I could hear and feel the soul," said Bobby.

Once again, Bobby just knew that God had put him in the right place at the right time. He had the opportunity to play with T. G. Sheppard on all of his number one hits. T. G. had that unique, soulful sound that just fit with what Bobby always looked for in a recording session. This conversation was just another reminder of the special artists that had been brought into his life and the blessings gained from having the opportunity to work together.

## Chapter Twenty-Nine

THE HIGHWAYMEN

Chips Moman introduced Bobby to Willie Nelson while they were in Pedernales, Texas. Bobby was there to work on an album for Willie. Willie had been around for quite some time. He had and still has a voice like no other. It's unique and people like to just hear Willie sing the way that only he can.

Bobby had the opportunity to work with Willie and Merle Haggard on "Pancho and Lefty." This was a very successful venture. So much so that the next track that Bobby played on with Willie Nelson was "Always On My Mind."

Willie was always laid back. He knew that it would work out however it should. That's probably one reason he is so successful. He is true to his roots. "City of New Orleans" came onto the scene, and Willie had another hit.

Then, Chips Moman came up with the idea to create an album called *The Highwaymen*. Jimmy Webb pitched the song, "Highwayman" to Chips. Webb was a mega-writer that also wrote "MacArthur Park" and "By the Time I Get to Phoenix," along with many others.

Chips wanted to get Johnny Cash, Waylon Jennings, Willie Nelson, and Merle Haggard to do the album. Merle declined the offer. Johnny Cash was a good friend of Kris Kristofferson, and Kris became the fourth member of The Highwaymen.

This was an unusual situation in that you had four megastars in one recording studio. But all of these guys had a mutual respect for each other. They showcased their own talents, but at times you could feel a little of the competition between them. The bottom line was that they each did what they had to do to make a song work, including stepping up to a new and different level. The goal was to do an album about outlaws. They were all considered "outlaws" in their own right. They did not do things the "Nashville" way. But it was that uniqueness that made each of them great.

The Highwaymen along with Chips and the Memphis Boys went into the studio and recorded *The Highwaymen* album. This first album was a major hit. A second album appropriately named *The Highwaymen 2* was also recorded. The public loved hearing these living legends.

Chips suggested that the Highwaymen go on tour. Discussions took place regarding which musicians to use. Chips suggested that they use the studio band and everyone agreed that this was the right thing to do. The extra band members were Mickey Raffeal (who was Willie Nelson's) harmonica player, Danny Tims (who was Kris Kristofferson's keyboard player), Robby Turner on steel guitar and J.R. Cobb from the Atlanta Rhythm Section. Bobby, J.R., and Danny would also sing background. Before they began the first American tour, they took the buses and went to Scottsdale, Arizona, where they rehearsed for one week.

With a nine-piece band and the four Highwaymen, there were thirteen instruments on stage. Chips suggested that each band member play only on the songs of which they had been a part. Otherwise, it would have been a nightmare for everybody to be playing at once, not to mention the challenges that it would present for the engineer. For the Memphis Boys and Chips, they were adamant that the songs sounded exactly like the records. That's what the fans paid for and expected to hear. The fans were loyal. In fact, there were groups of fans that traveled anywhere just to hear this legendary group.

These four superstars came together, and, along with the band, entertained audiences all over the United States Europe and Australia for three years. There were also multiple Las Vegas shows at the Mirage. Those shows were booked for a week at a time and were always sold out.

When those four men would enter the stage, the band set the mood. The audiences went wild. Here were four living legends with a legendary band. What a sound!

Kris Kristofferson would sing his big hit, "Why Me, Lord." The audiences loved it. A crowd favorite for Waylon Jennings was "Lukenbach, Texas." The Willie Nelson crowd pleaser was "Always On My Mind." Johnny Cash could begin with "Hello, I'm Johnny Cash." The audience would erupt with enthusiasm. "Folsom Prison" was the icing on the cake.

Johnny Cash was king in Europe. He was known as one of the Sun Studio artists. Europeans were high on Sun Recording artists. But this entire group had a large following. However, as the story goes, the fans loved the Highwaymen, but they also embraced the band. Fans would wait for the artists and the band to come off the stage. The accolades really flowed. Fans loved the performing artists and the musicians who played with them.

## Chapter Thirty

TRUE LEGENDS

Bobby has worked with true legends. The album, *Class of '55*, consisted of Johnny Cash, Carl Perkins, Jerry Lee Lewis and Roy Orbison. At one point in time all of these artists were on the Sun record label.

The album was released through Chips Moman's American Sound Studios and Smash Records. These Sun record stars had already found their place in music history. Besides the four main artists, the last song on the album was "Big Train" (from Memphis). Background voices on this song included Ricky Nelson, June Carter Cash, The Judds, John Fogerty, and Dave Edmonds. This was the last recording session for Ricky Nelson before his untimely death on December 31, 1985. The album was released in 1986 and received a Grammy. It was the only Grammy for Ricky Nelson's career.

One real privilege for Bobby was working with Dolly Parton. Dolly had already placed her stamp on music history. With Dolly, you get a reality check. What you see is what you get. She is the real deal. She is bubbly all the time. For Bobby, she is one of his all-time favorite singers. She is loaded with talent. She can sing any kind of music, and she knows how to deliver a song. She knows and appreciates a good song when she hears it.

On a television interview she said, "If a great song crosses my desk that I didn't have anything to do with, and it's something that I can do, I will record it."

Dolly Parton was a great writer. She was one of the few people that had a natural, God-given talent for writing songs. That's smart business and Dolly is "street smart." Bottom line, Dolly is one of music's greatest legends.

George Jones usually recorded songs written by other people. Bobby was acoustic piano player for "He Stopped Loving Her Today," which was his biggest record ever. George did not like the song too much. In fact, he made a bet with Billy Sherrill that the song would not be a number-one hit. George lost the bet.

George was a laid back guy. When he agreed to do the "Beer Run" song with Garth Brooks, George came to the studio, but was not getting into the groove of the song. George called Billy Sherrill and told him about the song, so Billy listened to the song and told him, "George, you have got to treat this song like white lightening and have fun with it."

George listened to Billy because he could always help George refocus. George took Billy's advice and went into the studio. The song was done on the first take. Bobby had played on the "Beer Run" track. When he heard the final product with the overdub of George's voice, he knew that was another hit!

As time went on, Bobby worked with Waylon Jennings while at Chips Moman's studio in Nashville. Bobby played on a number of Waylon's records.

Brenda Lee recorded in Memphis in the early days to work with Chips and the 827 Thomas Street Band. Although the album was not one of her greatest hits, she has always said that working with the Memphis group was one of the highlights of her career.

Billy Sherrill did an album with various artists including Barbara Mandrell, Hank Williams, Jr., George Jones, Willie Nelson, and Ray Charles. The song sung by Willie and Ray was 'Seven Spanish Angels' and ended up as a hit at the top of the charts. Bobby played piano for this project with Billy. Bobby continued to etch his name in music history, aligning himself with songs of legends.

Bobby's personality allows him to work well with all of the artists. He has always said that everyone has his or her own talents and abilities. He has learned to accept each person as an individual. But he has remained true to his principles, his creativity, his commitments and his faith.

## Chapter Thirty-One

### THE DESIRE TO WRITE

Bobby learned early on that if you have a good idea then other writers are willing to work with you. Bobby's strength in a song has always been not only the idea, but the melody and groove, from "Half the Way" to "Talkin' In Your Sleep" and "Commitment."

He has always been able to combine his talents with those who balance him out with the lyrics. He believes that you must have that perfect combination. Lyrics alone are not enough. In Europe, if you listen to the songs, you will find them to be very melodic. The songs that have been worldwide have always had great melodies.

When Bobby first moved to Nashville in 1972, he realized that Nashville was a songwriting town. As soon as you turn on to Sixteenth Avenue, you could feel the creativity. It is the same thing as when you go to Hollywood. You can feel the spirit of acting. In Nashville you can feel the spirit of writing.

Johnny Christopher, a close friend of Bobby's, had already experienced hits in Memphis. He and Bobby were together a lot and found themselves writing together quite often. After Bobby and Johnny had co-written Bobby's first number one hit "Still Thinking About You" sung by Crash Craddock, Bobby really had the bug to write. Shortly after that time, Roger Cook and Bobby got together had co-written "What's Your Name, What's Your Number?" for Andrea True and the Love Connection. This was a disco hit.

Other writing ventures led to hits like:

"Your Love Still Brings Me to My Knees' recorded in thirteen languages around the world.

"Talkin' in Your Sleep" co-written with Roger Cook and recorded by Crystal Gayle.

"Half the Way" co-written with Ralph Murphy and recorded by Crystal Gayle.

"He Got You" co-written with Ralph Murphy and recorded by Crystal Gayle.

"Better Love Next Time" co-written with Johnny Christopher and recorded by Merle Haggard.

"Always Was" co-written with Tony Colton and recorded by Aaron Tippen.

"In Another's Eyes" co-written with Garth Brooks and recorded by Garth Brooks and Trisha Yearwood.

"Commitment" co-written with Tony Colton and recorded by LeAnn Rimes.

"Don't Tell Me You're Not In Love" co-written by Tony Colton and Kim Williams and recorded by George Strait.

Bobby says, "Every person that you write with will always be different. You must adapt to every situation. You have to determine if they are more musical or more lyrical and go from there."

Bobby finds that he does better with lyrical people since he is more melodic and can feel the groove.

Roger Cook approached Bobby and asked him to write with Ralph Murphy, who was just coming in to Picalic. Bobby and Ralph got together and Bobby determined very quickly that

Ralph was more lyrical.

The pair went into one of the writer's rooms, Bobby sat down at the piano and began to play a groove that had come to him. At one point during that work session, the title 'Don't Take Me Half the Way' came to Bobby's mind. Ralph suggested that Bobby hum the melody to the verses and chorus and they would put it on tape. Ralph took the tape home with him that afternoon.

Ralph lived in Mount Juliet, which was about 30 minutes from Nashville. On the ride home, he put the tape in his car cassette player and listened to it. He came in the next day with the lyrics finished. They went into the studio and made a demo of the song. The title was shortened to "Half the Way." Allen Reynolds heard the song and wanted it for Crystal Gayle.

During those days, the song would be played for the producer. They would then take the song and play it for the artist. If the artist liked the song, then the producer would call the publisher and put it on hold. Sometimes this process could take as long as six months.

One day Johnny Christopher came over to Picalic with a song that he had started. He only had a melody for the entrance to his song. He asked Bobby to come up with something for a chorus. They were in the office next door to Ralph. When Bobby came up with the chorus for the song, which they repeated several times, they ended up finishing the song that same day.

Ralph came in the next day and said, "I hate you!"

He said that he had stayed awake all night singing the chorus of this song that Bobby and Johnny had written together. It was called "Better Love Next Time."

Writing allows creativity. Bobby has often said, "When you create a piece of work, going to the studio and watching it come to life, is one of the greatest feelings a person could ever have. Nothing else I can think of, including being on the road, compares to the creativity of the music business."

# Chapter Thirty-Two

ON THE ROAD—IN THE STUDIO

A part of Bobby's success comes from the fact that he has been exposed to several facets of the music. Playing on the road becomes rote. The musicians play night after night, and they are playing what was created in the studio.

In the studio, a masterpiece is being created. Creativity is at its finest point. The creativity and fine-tuning will make or break the song. It will mean the difference between a smash hit and another record for the shelf. The studio is another world. You have to have a natural feel to know exactly what goes on the song.

Ego cannot come into play. Bobby is never afraid to step back, to lay out on any song. The focus for Bobby has always been the end result—what compliments the artist and as well as the song.

To begin to name all of the hits tied to Bobby Wood's name would be impossible. While this list may be short, it highlights some of Bobby's major successes. There are over tens of thousands of recordings from fifty years of music history.

*Beyond the Season* Album (Garth Brooks)

"Double Live" Album (Garth Brooks)
"Fresh Horses" Album (Garth Brooks)
"Garth Brooks" Album (Garth Brooks)
"In Pieces" Album (Garth Brooks)
"Limited Series Box Set" Album (Garth Brooks)
"Magic of Christmas" Album (Garth Brooks)
"No Fences" Album (Garth Brooks)
"Ropin' the Wind" Album (Garth Brooks)
"Scarecrow" Album (Garth Brooks)
"Sevens" Album (Garth Brooks)
"The Chase" Album (Garth Brooks)
"The Hits" Album (Garth Brooks)
"The Lost Sessions" Album (Garth Brooks)
"Elvis in Memphis" Album (Elvis Presley)
"I Believe: The Gospel Masters (Elvis Presley)
"Elvis—Back in Memphis" Album (Elvis Presley)
"Suspicious Minds" (Elvis Presley)
"In the Ghetto" (Elvis Presley)
"Kentucky Rain" (Elvis Presley)
"Don't Cry Daddy" (Elvis Presley)
"Mr. Bojangles" (Jerry Jeff Walker)
"If I'm A Fool For Loving You" (Bobby Wood)
"Little Red Riding Hood" (Sam the Sham)
"For Your Precious Love" (Oscar Tony, Jr.)
"Windmills of Your Mind" (Dusty Springfield)
"Hooked on a Feeling" (B.J. Thomas)
"I Just Can't Help Believing" (B.J. Thomas)
"Rings" (Cymarron)
"Sweet Caroline" (Neil Diamond)
"Brother Love" (Neil Diamond)
"Holly Holy" (Neil Diamond)
"The Essential Roy Orbison" (Roy Orbison)
"Angel of the Morning" (Merrilee Rush)

"Skinny Legs" (Joe Tex)
"I Gottcha" (Joe Tex)
"Good Time Charlie" (Danny O"Keefe)
"Midnight Mover" (Wilson Pickett)
"I"m In Love" (Wilson Pickett)
"Wilson Pickett: A Man An A Half" (Wilson Pickett)
"Memphis Soul Stew" (King Curtis)
"Why Me, Lord" (Kris Kristofferson)
"Golden Rings" (George Jones and Tammy Wynette)
"Somebody Done Somebody Wrong Song" (B.J. Thomas)
"Lucille" (Kenny Rogers)
"Kenny Rogers/Kenny" (Kenny Rogers)
"Talkin' In Your Sleep" (Crystal Gayle)
"Half the Way" (Crystal Gayle)
"You Look So Good In Love" (George Strait)
"Fort Worth" (George Strait)
"Everlasting Love" (Carl Carlton)
"Highwayman" (Johnny Cash, Willie Nelson, Kris Kristofferson, Waylon Jennings)
"Highwayman 2" (Johnny Cash, Willie Nelson, Kris Kristofferson, Waylon Jennings)
"Always On My Mind" (Willie Nelson)
"City of New Orleans" (Willie Nelson)
"The Great American Songbook" (WillieNelson)
"Johnny Cash Is Coming to Town/Water from the Wells of Home" (Johnny Cash)
"Pancho and Lefty" (Merle Haggard and Willie Nelson)
"Nashville Rebel" (Waylon Jennings)
"I Can Help" (Billy Swan)
"He Stopped Loving Her Today" (George Jones)
"My Very Special Guests" (George Jones)
"Seven Spanish Angels" (Ray Charles and Willie Nelson)
"Images" (Ronnie Milsap)

"There Ain't No Gettin'" Over Me" (Ronnie Millsap)
"1982" (Randy Travis)
"Memphis Underground" (Herbie Mann)
"Introducing Herbie Mann" (Herbie Mann)
"In Another's Eyes" (Garth Brooks and Trisha Yearwood)
"Sixteenth Avenue" (Lacy J. Dalton)
"Songbird: Rare Tracks and Forgotten Gems" (Emmylou Harris)
"All the Gold in California" (Gatlin Brothers)
"That's the Way Love Goes" (Merle Haggard)
"The Essential Merle Haggard: The Epic Years" (Merle Haggard)
"Unforgettable Merle Haggard" (Merle Haggard)
"Class of '55" (Roy Orbison, Jerry Lee Lewis, Johnny Cash, Carl Perkins)
"Pride and Joy: A Gospel Music Collection" (Charley Pride)
"Comfort Of Her Wings" (Charley Pride)
"You've Lost That Loving Feeling" (Dionne Warwick)
"Prime Prine" (John Prine)
"The Conway Twitty Collection" (Conway Twitty)
"Life's Like Poetry" (Lefty Frizzell)
"The Memphis Boys" (Bobby Wood, Bobby Emmons, Reggie Young, Gene Chrisman, Mike Leech)

# Chapter Thirty-Three

### THE MEMPHIS BOYS TODAY

Bobby Wood is still playing with the Memphis Boys today. Artists in the United States and abroad count it a privilege to perform with this renowned group of talented individuals. Garth Brooks deemed Bobby "one of the most creative keyboard players." Elvis Presley was quoted as saying that Bobby Wood is the most commercial piano player he ever knew.

The Memphis Boys, as a group, are performing worldwide. Their European fan base continues to grow. Their shows are all sell-out shows. The fans know them by name. In the United States, people continue to buy their records. Sometimes they know who the band is behind the artist, and sometimes they don't. But they know talent and they know quality when they hear it.

On November 26, 2007, the Memphis Boys were one of the first studio groups to be inducted into the Musicians' Hall of Fame at the Schermerhorn Symphony Center in downtown Nashville. Ballots were distributed and the voting included music professional from all genres of music. An advisory board determined the inductees. Garth Brooks introduced the Memphis Boys and performed "Suspicious Minds" with the band. A sold-out crowd was present and music lovers got to hear some of their favorite artists as well as the people behind them.

Bobby recently said, "You know, for a bunch of old guys, it is amazing that we can still draw a crowd."

It shouldn't be surprising. The heart and soul of the music is still there. They have set sales records, sold more music, had more number one hits, and have touched many genres of music. They are still the best.

## Chapter Thirty-Four

One of the most frequently asked questions for Bobby is, "How many famous people have you really recorded or worked with in your music history?"

I am not sure that even Bobby has the answer to that question. As he pondered throughout his career, he was able to come up with some of the notable names. This list is far from inclusive of everyone, but it gives a picture of the talent of the man on the keyboard.

| | |
|---|---|
| Anderson, John | Bramlett, Bonnie |
| Andrews, Julie | Brooks, Garth |
| Arnold, Eddy | Buffet, Jimmy |
| Atkins, Chet | Burke, Solomon |
| Barbara and the Browns | Cale, J.J. |
| Bare, Bobby | Cannon, Ace |
| Baxter, Skunk | Carlton, Carl |
| Bland, Bobby Blue | Carr, James |
| Blossoms | Cash, Johnny |
| Box Tops | Charles, Ray |

Clark, Petula
Clement, Jack
Coe, David Allen
Coffee, Dennis
Cotton, Gene
Curtis, King
Cymarron
Dalton, Lacy J.
Davis, Jimmy
Day, Doris
Diamond, Neil
Dorman, Harold
Duvall, Robert
Eddie, Duane
Everly Brothers
Frizzel, Lefty
Gatlin Brothers
Gayle, Crystal
Gibbons, Billy
Gibson, Don
Gilley, Mickey
Goldsboro, Bobby
Grant, Amy
Greenwood, Lee
Haggard, Merle
Haley, Bill
Harris, Emmylou
Hall, Tom T.
Henry, Clarence Frogman
Highwaymen
Hinds, Chrisie
Jennings, Waylon
Jones, George

Jones, Grandpa
King, B.B.
Kristofferson, Kris
Lee, Brenda
Lewis, Huey
Lewis, Jerry Lee
Lukather, Steve
Lynn, Loretta
Mack, Lonnie
Mandrell, Barbara
Mann, Herbie
Mathis, Johnny
Mattea, Kathy
McClinton, Delbert
McDowell, Ronny
McIntire, Reba
Medley, Bill
Merchant, Natalie
Millsap, Ronnie
Moore, Scotty
Murphy, Michael Martin
Nelson, Ricky
Nelson, Willie
O'Keefe, Danny
Orbison, Roy
Ovations
Paul, Les
Parton, Dolly
Perkins, Carl
Piazza, Marguerite
Pickett, Wilson
Posey, Sandy
Presley, Elvis

Pride, Charlie
Prine, John
Purify Brothers
Reynolds, Burt
Rich, Charlie
Riley, Billy Lee
Rogers, Kenny
Royal, Billy Joe
Rush, Merrilee
Sambora, Richie
Sam the Sham
Seals, Dan
Sheppard, T.G.
Simon, Joe
Skaggs, Ricky
Slash
Snow, Hank
Springfield, Dusty
Starr, Ringo
Statler Brothers
Stewart, Gary

Strait, George
Swan, Billy
Tex, Joe
Thomas, B.J.
Tillis, Mel
Tony Jr., Oscar
Tucker, Tanya
Twitty, Conway
Travis, Randy
Wagoner, Porter
Walker, Jerry Jeff
Wariner, Steve
Warwick, Dionne
Wells, Kitty
White, Tony Joe
Williams, Don
Williams Jr., Hank
Womack, Bobby
Wynette, Tammy
Yearwood, Trisha

# *Epilogue*

Another stage. Another show.

Once again they hear the roar of the crowd. Now they are chanting—"Memphis—Memphis—Memphis." And just like many other times, the Memphis Boys enter the stage. Reggie Young, Mike Leech, Gene Chrisman, Bobby Wood, and Bobby Emmons. And just like all of the times before, the crowd erupts into thunderous applause.

The Memphis Boys look out at the packed theater. New faces are there. Familiar faces are there. But there is no lack of enthusiasm with anyone. The show begins, and the crowd jumps to their feet. No one sits down and no one leaves. Song by song the crowd claps and sings along.

Bobby can speak with confidence about the music business because of his association through the years with mega producers, artists, and musicians. Bobby will tell you he has been greatly blessed to work with great people who will always be called his friends. There are people like Sam Phillips, Chips Moman, Stan Kesler, Jack "Cowboy" Clement, Allen Reynolds, Jerry Wexler,

Ahmet Ertifgan, Arrif Mardin, Tom Dowd, Billy Sherrill, Papa Don Schroder, Tommy Cogbill, Owen Bradley, Buddy Killen, Fred Foster, Roy Dea, Chet Atkins, Jerry Crutchfield, Chip Young, and the list goes on. He will never forget the legendaries like Elvis and Garth. Then there are those guys who helped create that special sound, the sound of the Memphis Boys—Gene Chrisman, Bobby Emmons, Mike Leech, and Reggie Young. Add to that magical list the "G" men—Bruce Bouton, Mark Casstevens, Mike Chapman, Rob Hajacos, Chris Leuzinger, and Milton Sledge.

There have been over 200 million records sold that Bobby Wood has recorded on or been involved with through writing, producing, or other means.

In retrospect Bobby looks back at his life and what he has learned. He will be the first to tell you that he is to forgive as he has been forgiven by the grace of God.

Bobby puts it this way, "The preacher that embarrassed me as a teenager also taught me a lot as a grown up. He was a good man and preached what he believed to be true."

Only in later years would Bobby come to understand that none of us are perfect and only by the grace of God can we make it. After four years of drugs and living on the wild side, Bobby came to the realization that he was responsible for his own actions. You can only serve one master. When he made the decision to be more Christ-like, to make Him his master, he began to have the peace that passes all understanding. It's a peace that only God can give. It's the life that God wants us to show to the world.

Bobby says it this way, "I learned a long time ago that you have to develop an attitude of learning and teamwork. It doesn't matter who comes up with the idea; if it's good then everybody benefits." He continues, "I have found a few nuggets that I have held on to in my career. One is that when you stop learning you are either standing still or going backwards. The other jewel is that it just doesn't matter how much success you have. The day you start believing your own press is the day you forget the work ethics that got you there."

For Bobby, this has been the difference between enjoying life and not being bored with it.

Musicians who have worked with Bobby sit back in disbelief as they try to describe his unbelievable legacy. He's been described as a musician's musician.

But as the guy from Mitchell Switch, Mississippi, looks around, he says to himself, "I am so glad I never lost the dream. I am living my dream. And I am not finished yet."